STORIES OF THE STRANGE AND SINISTER

Frank Baker was born in London in 1908. From a young age, he had a deep interest in church music, serving as a chorister at Winchester Cathedral as a boy from 1919 to 1924. From 1924 to 1929, Baker worked as a marine insurance clerk in the City of London, an experience that he later fictionalized in *The Birds* (1936). He resigned in 1929 to take on secretarial work at an ecclesiastical music school where he hoped to make a career of music; during this time he also worked as a church organist.

He soon abandoned his musical studies and went to St. Just, on the west coast of Cornwall, where he became organist of the village church and lived alone in a stone cottage. It was during this time that he began writing; his first novel, *The Twisted Tree*, was published in 1935 by Peter Davies after nine other publishers rejected it. It was well received by critics, and its modest success prompted Baker to continue writing. In 1936, he published *The Birds*, which sold only about 300 copies and which its author described as 'a failure'. Nonetheless, after the release of Alfred Hitchcock's popular film of the same name in 1963, *The Birds* was reissued in paperback by Panther and received new attention. Baker's most successful and enduring work was *Miss Hargreaves* (1940), a comic fantasy in which two young people invent a story about an elderly woman, only to find that their imagination has in fact brought her to life.

During the Second World War, Baker became an actor and toured Britain before getting married in 1943 to Kathleen Lloyd, with whom he had three children. Baker continued to write, publishing more than a dozen more books, including *Mr. Allenby Loses the Way* (1945), *Embers* (1946), *My Friend the Enemy* (1948) and *Talk of the Devil* (1956). Baker died in Cornwall of cancer in 1983.

BY FRANK BAKER

FICTION

The Twisted Tree (1935)

The Birds (1936)

Miss Hargreaves (1940)

Allanayr (1941)

Sweet Chariot (1942)

Mr. Allenby Loses the Way (1945)

Before I Go Hence (1946)

Embers (1946)

The Downs So Free (1948)

My Friend the Enemy (1948)

Lease of Life (1954)

Talk of the Devil (1956)

Teresa: A Journey Out of Time (1960)

Stories of the Strange and Sinister (1983)

NONFICTION/AUTOBIOGRAPHICAL

The Road Was Free (1948)

I Follow But Myself (1968)

The Call of Cornwall (1976)

FRANK BAKER

Stories of the Strange and Sinister

With a new introduction by
R. B. RUSSELL

VALANCOURT BOOKS

Dedication: For David Simeon

Stories of the Strange and Sinister by Frank Baker
First published by William Kimber in 1983
First Valancourt Books edition 2016

'Art Thou Languid?' was first published in *At Close of Eve* edited by
Jeremy Scott (Jarrolds, 1947); 'The Green Steps' in *Cornish Harvest*
(1974), 'In the Steam Room' in *Stories of the Macabre* (1976), 'The
Sack' in *Stories of Horror* (1977), 'The Chocolate Box' in *Haunted
Cornwall* (1973), and 'Tyme Tryeth Troth' in *Stories of the Supernatural,*
(1979) all edited by Denys Val Baker and published by William Kimber.

Published by Valancourt Books, Richmond, Virginia
http://www.valancourtbooks.com

ISBN 978-1-943910-30-4 (trade hardcover)
ISBN 978-1-943910-31-1 (trade paperback)
Also available as an electronic book.

All Valancourt Books publications are printed on acid free paper
that meets all ANSI standards for archival quality paper.

Cover by M. S. Corley
Set in Bembo

INTRODUCTION

It is not good enough to simply be a good writer. For an author to achieve any kind of recognisable literary success, be it critical or popular, contemporary or posthumous, so many planets must align that only the smallest percentage of authors will ever be literary stars. For Frank Baker the celestial bodies never quite lined up in the night sky, although they often came tantalisingly close.

At his best Frank Baker could write very well, with sympathetic and believable characters, an endearing lightness of touch and a quietly understated humour which means that his novel *Miss Hargreaves* (1940) is nothing less than a masterpiece. It is one of very, very few books that successfully combines humour and horror. (These elements almost always undermine each other.) With his title character, Frank Baker created a monster every bit as frightening and dangerous as the creation of Shelley's Victor Frankenstein, yet Miss Hargreaves observes all the social niceties and even writes poetry reminiscent of Edward Lear. Literary astronomers would have noted that the inimitable Margaret Rutherford successfully played the part of Miss Hargreaves on the London stage; a casting match made in heaven. Had the Second World War not intervened then a classic British comedy might have been filmed that would have stood proudly alongside *A School for Scoundrels* or *The Ladykillers*, immortalising the name of Frank Baker. However, world events conspired against him, and the final planet refused to align.

In the second half of the twentieth century the big screen was a sure-fire way of reaching huge audiences and thereby selling books and gaining fame. Baker might have had a second chance if the planets had decided to take pity on him, but they didn't: when Alfred Hitchcock decided to make *The Birds* he chose to adapt Daphne du Maurier's 1952 short story, not Baker's earlier novel of the same title. Baker was convinced that he had been cheated, for du Maurier's story of avian attacks on humans is essentially the same as his. However, Baker was a musician at heart and often wrote his fiction in a minor key. This was a great counterpoint to the larger-than-life character of Miss Hargreaves, but it was not appropriate for *The Birds*. His ponderously-told novel meant that only a few hundred copies were sold, and Hitchcock inevitably alighted on du Maurier's work rather than his. Baker could not argue with this, but he was convinced he had been plagiarised by du Maurier. The fact that she was the cousin of his publisher, Peter Davies, was not proof that would stand up in court, and with hindsight it appears unlikely to have happened the way he imagined. Baker's sense of injustice seems to have temporarily caused him to forget that his own book was directly inspired by Arthur Machen's *The Terror*, and if du Maurier had stolen Baker's story, then credit for Hitchcock's classic film should probably have gone to Machen.

There are elements in Baker's writing that might have made for other memorable books, but they never quite coalesced harmoniously. For instance, *Allanayr* (reprinted as *Full Score*) tells the story of a minor composer and contains passages of quiet delight and beauty. It was the perfect subject matter for Baker, but his characters are pleasant under-achievers, and the book never quite transcends the mundanity of their lives and situations. While Oscar Wilde was in the gutter looking up at the stars, and Arthur Machen dreamed in fire but worked in clay, perhaps Frank Baker never quite set his sights high enough? (*Miss Hargreaves* was an exception, of course; a 'force of nature' who will have demanded of the author that her story be told.)

Stories of the Strange and Sinister reflects both Baker's strengths and weaknesses as a writer. He describes his fellow man with sympathy and understanding and makes him believable. In 'Art Thou Languid?' Baker's depiction of the quiet tragedy of everyday life is understated but powerful, and the question of a haunting almost need not have arisen. At his best, Baker, like the author of *Lolly Willowes*, Sylvia Townsend Warner, makes the point that apparently ordinary people can be remarkable, and the finest story in this collection, 'My Lady Sweet, Arise' is a delightful fantasy that could have come from the pen of Warner at her most playful. It suggests that the 'strange', now called the 'weird', was perhaps Baker's strength. He was, perhaps, less successful with his 'sinister' stories: 'The Chocolate Box' and 'The Steam Room' have a certain grim interest, but 'The Sack', which ought to offer a number of unnerving moments, is let down by the pun that appears at the beginning of the tale and is never quite shaken off.

But 'Quintin Claribel' may be the story that remains longest in the reader's mind. It is quite absurd, but it has the plausibility of those nightmares that we never seem to wake up from soon enough. Perhaps it was the 'absurd' that was Baker's métier, rather than the 'strange' or 'sinister', but even if Baker had realised this and had written more in this vein, one can't help thinking that the planets would still have not done him any favours.

R. B. Russell
January 2016

R. B. Russell is an English author, born in Sussex, and the co-proprietor of the independent publishing house Tartarus Press, which he runs with his partner Rosalie Parker. He has had three collections of his own short stories published, *Putting the Pieces in Place* (2009), *Literary Remains* (2010) and *Leave Your Sleep* (2012); a novella, *Bloody Baudelaire* (2009), and a collected edition, *Ghosts* (2012).

CONTENTS

The Green Steps	3
My Lady Sweet, Arise	20
The Sack	42
Art Thou Languid?	54
The Chocolate Box	81
Quintin Claribel	97
In the Steam Room	125
Flowers I Leave You	136
Coombe Morwen	147
Tyme Tryeth Troth	163

I

The Green Steps

The man who sweeps the narrow twisting streets and alley-ways in our village, is he human? Has he a story, has he past and future like other people? Or has he only the present? Is he time, sweeping away our withered illusions? – the drift and dross of our leaflike years, the potato parings, the tattered bits of old newspapers, envelopes, cigarette cartons, paid and unpaid accounts, drawn by his long stiff brush into the shovel and thus to the little cart to be wheeled away by him, as evening comes, to the rubbish dump, the waste land in a stony valley overhung by frowning, glowering woods behind the village.

Whenever I encounter him I think of the finger of fate, of something that awaits us all that we least expect, of a sign-post on the moor when we cannot turn back. I think of the sad great songs of Schubert, and the tormented starlike inno-cence of Hans Andersen, of Don Quixote reborn without the desire to tilt at windmills. And yet he is a kindly man. One sees that at once. His long, lean, spindly figure; his shuffling, minc-ing gait; his knuckly, fumbling fingers; his thin nose and chin that seem to want to close like a pair of pincers; his opaque, chestnut-coloured eyes; his frostbitten fortitude – all these give an air of detached and consecrated beneficence. That man couldn't hurt a fly, one would say. If a living fly were struggling on a flypaper in the road, and the stiff brush bristled towards it, the Scavenger would make a detour, avoiding the victim, and probably pick up the wounded fly, take it home, feed it, tend it, train it to understand the cruelty in the world and go out again, aware of flypapers and all that comes between flies and their heaven. That is the sort of man he is, you would say. And you guess that he has suffered much, seen much, seen some

3

visions perhaps, knows many secrets, embraced scavenging as the last symbol of man's destiny. Back to dust before his time this man seems to wish to go. Or is he working off a long penance, bowed down by an old crime against humanity?

This is more near to the truth, though not all of it; for this man was once a murderer. I have got his story and I will tell it to you.

I had observed him often and I had good reason to know where he lived, for it was very close to our cottage, up the cliff path, that bends sharply uphill over the harbour and the boatmasts that swing and sway in the gales; a path too narrow for any traffic, with rows of cottages, different sizes, shapes and colours, on one side. From the windows of our living-room which overlooks an area – a waste bit of land where kids keep rabbits in hutches and women dry clothes and men saw wood in the winter – I would often, and still often see, the Scavenger. Above the area there are steps, the Green Steps they are called, worn away dangerously, all uneven, ground by the feet of many generations, the stone crumbling, little weeds growing from the cracks. I'd always had a curious familiar feeling about the Green Steps; they brought back a hint of the past to me, a paragraph of my boyhood, as though I'd been there years ago; and I knew I hadn't. Then, it seemed to me, it was just the name – the Green Steps – that carried some old memory I couldn't place. Anyway, there Robert Starling the Scavenger lived, up the Green Steps; and on moonless nights, however familiar you were with those few steps (there are only about five, or seven; one can never count straight, they seem to change their number every day) you were likely to lose your footing and tumble backward, or forward. Up to a grassy hill-side sloped over harbour and sea and village roofs, the steps ascend; to a drying-ground where on Monday mornings pants and shirts and socks and pyjamas and overalls and exuberant nightdresses billow and flutter in the dry east wind; a happy place, where little boys play wild games of Touch and Bang-you're-dead, and little girls nurse dollies and dress up like the Queen of

Egypt. (I saw one once; she was swathed with bright-coloured stuffs pinched from an old drawer of Mother's; a kid of about eight, and when I asked her who she thought she was, she said Cleopatra.)

These dangerous steps ascend between cottages built on all levels that overhang courtyards where the fishermen dry nets and make baskets from willows. A very narrow passageway it is; always something of an effort to get up there at night or when the rain gushes down and the wind slashes you round a corner. Every late afternoon when his job was finished, Robert Starling climbed up there and drifted down again in the very early morning to gather up another day's débris. He lived in one of the cottages opening on to the passage, a very old place, with the rain streaming in where slates had clattered off the roof, slates that he himself swept next day into his little cart. It was when I watched him sweeping those slates of his, gathering up his own protection against the elements, that I first spoke to him. There was something grim and yet humorous about his expression, as though he knew just what he was doing. I talked about it having been a terrible wild night, to which he agreed; and I went on to say that he'd have to get into touch with his landlord to do something about the roof. To which he only shrugged his shoulders.

I made some inquiries. It appeared there wasn't a landlord. Starling had taken over the cottage years and years ago from an old man whose wife had died and who didn't want to use it any more. Then the old man had died in the workhouse, the children had emigrated, as Cornishmen do, far away to mines in search of gold; Starling lived on in the cottage, never paying any rent, and nobody bothered him. In our village people talk about you and invent tales about you; but ultimately they leave you alone. You can go to heaven or hell your own way, blow your nose on your sleeve or use the best silver teapot to shave from. Nobody really cares. We live on the sea and the sea blows into the harbour and over the walls in the high spring tides and seeps and sucks its way into the narrow streets. Plundering this sea, fishermen live perilous and precarious lives and nobody believes in that great civilized myth, Security. Everybody's their own destiny, and if Robert Starling chose to live alone for twenty-five years in a two-roomed cottage that was slowly falling down, let him do so. Bob Starling was accepted as part of the village, and no more questions were asked about him.

But I wanted to know more. He tormented me, trudging so primly up the steps every late afternoon, so far away in a world of his own, like a figure in a story book come to life. So I asked our neighbour, Jack Williams, about him. Jack is a fisherman and there is little he doesn't know about everybody, new or old, in the village. So when I said, 'Jack, tell me something about old Bob Starling,' out came a lot, but not enough, nothing quite hung together.

'Oh, old Starling, he'm as mad as a hare, yet there's nothing that man couldn't do if he chose. I don't know what he hasn't done in days gone by. He's drove the fish lorry into market, he's served in shops, he's done window-cleaning, rat-snaring, wood-chopping, house-painting, coal-heaving. Time was, he used to write signs and letters for they who couldn't read nor write theirselves. Twenty-five years he's lived up Green Steps. He's got a room back there stacked with bits of paper full of fancy poems. Some of them was published, they do say. He had a woman once, pretty maid she were; but that were in his drinking days.'

'Drinking days?'

'Didn't you know old Starling used to be the biggest raging thirst in the town? There was nothing he wouldn't put away as a young man, crazy mad he used to get, shouting and swearing and singing up the steps. They say he'd fall on the paraffin can when nothing else was left. And all the time scribbling on bits of paper that used to flutter out of his pockets and drift about the square. Just words, he used to write. That man had more words in his head than the sea's got fish. And he'd sing like a lark in they days, all the pretty old songs were ABC to him. Bob was a fine chap. But after he gone over cliff and landed up in the Infirmary, that were the end of en. He never drunk another drop and it didn't do him no good either. It lost him his woman, for one thing. What was the maid called, now? Stella, that's the name; and he used to call her his Star, said that was what the word meant. And she were like a star, too; shining, pretty, twinkling face she had, fit to break through any cloud in a man. But away she went and she's never come back. If she's alive and knows about him, I reckon if he were to start in on the drink again, she'd come back to en, she couldn't help it.'

'Did she drink too?'

'Just a bit, to keep Bob company, never much. But she liked en drunk, everybody did like Bob drunk, you couldn't help it. Even when he bashed her about a bit, she still loved en. Then one night, in one of his fits, he rushed up Green Steps – wild, roaring night it was, sea like heaving mountains over quay – he rushed up there like a whirlwind cursing black hell. He were chasing someone, he said. "I'll kill you," he was hollering, "I'll bash your brains out, I'll chuck you over cliff." God knows who he thought he was after. Anyway, over the cliff, up Battery, he went; and how he didn't break himself into little pieces isn't reasonable; but he didn't. I reckon Stella would've been glad, in a sense, if he had. He broke his leg and arm and bruised and cut himself something terrible, and had to be dragged up with ropes by the coastguard and me and other chaps. Took us all night. He'd landed twenty feet down on a bit of jutting-out rock; another inch and he'd have gone a hundred and fifty feet to the bottom and that'd been the finish of Bob Starling. But he were lucky. He spent about six months up to the Infirmary, and when he come back to Stella he were as quiet as Sunday morning. "I killed en," he kept saying. "I finished en off, Stella. He'm gone for ever." Poor maid couldn't make sense of en. No more strong drink for he. No more of they songs and poems. Job after job he takes and comes slinking home with his pay-packet till Stella could scream. Never any fun like the old days. That's why she left en. She was a high-spirited maid and wasn't born to bide with angels.'

'Wait a bit, wait a bit!' I cried. I had been half listening, half following another train of thought in my mind. And now at last I understood the significance (for me) of the Green Steps.

Going to a cupboard in my study where I keep piles of old literaries and periodicals, I searched for what I wanted: copies of
the *London Alchemist* for 1923-4.

'You say,' I said, 'that he published some of these poems of
his?'

'So they did say. There were lots of writing chaps around
here in those days, chaps with beards and coloured shirts. And
Bob were one of them.'

'Did he ever call himself *Robin* Starling?'

'Not Robin. No. It were always Bob.'

'Ah!' I gave an exclamation of triumph. I had found the
poem that had so vaguely yet so significantly lurched back into
my mind, lines that I had read years ago as a schoolboy. 'The
Green Steps,' it was called. It was about a scavenger who 'feeds
on wasted vision'. And it was by Robin Starling.

Well, I said to myself, when Jack Williams had gone presently
and I pondered over the strange lines of this forgotten old
poem of the neo-Georgians – tantalizing as it is to play with
the idea that this queer old scavenger is Robin Starling grown
old – it just will not do. For Robin Starling, a brief and brilliant voice in the early twenties, had died almost before his
evocative lyricism had had time to linger in the ear. By only a
few present-day critics would even his name be remembered.
And probably not one poem of about a dozen that got published in various literaries of the period would now be recalled
by anybody. Except me? Was I the only person who had been
moved by 'The Green Steps'? And had lingered over it in my
boyhood, feeling that it had a special meaning for me that I
only half understood? I had come across no other lines by this
poet; he had quite gone out of my mind; and now returned by
the strangest coincidence – that he bore almost the same name
and wrote about the Green Steps – and a scavenger.

But was this coincidence? I couldn't, of course, let it rest
here. Robin Starling was dead, that was pretty certain. For now
I recalled a brief obituary notice about him, that I couldn't
find in any of my old magazines. But, Jack Williams had said,

the Bob Starling of twenty-five years ago had written poems;
and he had tumbled over a cliff, apparently under the illusion
that he was chasing somebody. *Had it been an illusion?* Had this
old scavenger really been chasing somebody up the Green
Steps that dark wild night of twenty-five years ago? Had he – ?

Innumerable questions. The beginning of an exciting quest.
All simplified, you might say, by direct questions to the man
himself. Not so. For you could not get beyond that amber-like
glint in his eyes, and never any more than a few words would
he mutter to you, always courteous, always humble, but about
as talkative as a Trappist monk in Holy Week.

I thought about it endlessly. I read and re-read the strange,
sad, yet exciting poem. Not a very good poem as we would
think now. It made sense and it rhymed; but it said far more
under its simple words than a first reading made clear. Was I to
believe that this was not the work of the old man himself? A
room stacked with manuscripts, Jack Williams had said; and literary high-yap in the twenties, coloured shirts and beards and
Bloomsbury gone wild as Bloomsbury does once it goes west.

Two burning questions. How had 'Robin Starling' died?
And – had 'Bob Starling' actually been chasing somebody up
those steps?

The first question was easily answered. I wrote to a friend of
mine, a critic whose pleasure it is to ponder over the oddities
of literature – the forgotten ones who find their unlamented
way into the Charing Cross Road book troughs. What could
he tell me about Robin Starling?

The answer was terrifyingly what I had expected. Starling, after spending the early years of his life wandering about
France and England, a sort of Villon with ever a rabble of noisy
scoundrels at his heels, and ever a woman to worship him, had
written a handful of verse. Like Rimbaud he had become a
flame, rapidly to die out, yet kindle other sleeping fires. The
last two years of his life, said my friend, he had spent in the West
of England. 'You should know all about him' (I quote from
his letter), 'since he lived in your village and gathered a rusty-

fusty greenery-yallery crew around him. He went the whole
hog with drink and had, I believe, one faithful woman who
loved him; dead now, probably like him. His death was "cor-
rect". Dead drunk, he ran up a steep cliff path and smashed
himself to bits two hundred feet below. That was the story
put round by a brother of his, anyway; and this brother had
the handling of some poems published – only in the literaries
– shortly after his death; I believe he wrote one critical article
in praise of his work in a thing I now can't trace, an ephemera
of the middle twenties. Then the brother seems to have gone
silent, and all Starling's rackety set came to nothing. Starling's
was a brief, but certain trumpet note that died in the air before
anyone heard it properly. You should make it your business to
discover all you can about him. For all we know he might have
left a mass of work behind him that should see the light. Does
the brother still live, I wonder?'

O, my Scavenger, how dear you became to me! How lovingly
I studied you from that day, watching your devouring broom
over the sea-washed streets in the sleeping morning when
sometimes I rose early and walked to the harbour to see what
news lay in the east! How keenly I observed the sharp inward
curve of your nostrils, your fastidious yet workmanlike hands,
your shuffling yet ambassador walk! Like a man with a train of
princes behind him, all ghosts, you seemed to me. Bowing in
to life the great ones of the earth, and then waiting for them to
be flung out by the wind to drift in the streets and come under
the drag of your brush. Ushering in and gathering up, day by
day you assumed more importance for me. There was a major
work in you, I said. A major work for a novelist of supreme
imagination and superb craft. Henry James, Flaubert and Dos-
toevsky linked as one, could not do justice to you.

    For some time I made no attempt to gather up the threads
of the story. Good stories linger in the air like flower scents of
autumn smoke, about the tongue like wine, about the touch
like silk; and shift and struggle before the eyes like the ever-
changing patterns and colours seen through a child's kaleido-

scope. They do not mature in a hurry. Were I to rush forward and breast the tape of truth, should I indeed have won the truth? For truth is the whole tale, and had it yet ended? Had I, perhaps, to wait till the Scavenger died and the contents of that back room could be examined?

Then, one night, something very strange happened and I was suddenly dragged, as it were by the scruff of a too inquisitive neck, right into the heart of the tale. Now it is mine, gone for ever, and as I relate it, so it will cease to be his or mine. It will be anybody's, and anybody can learn what they like from it.

It was a night in January, after days of rain and gales, gales that battered the side of our cottage and made it sway like a ship in a full and roaring sea. A Moby Dick night; and the high spring tides seventeen feet up in the fifteen-foot harbour, the boats all swaying their masts like a wind-thrashed forest of leafless larches. The fishermen had been to the boats in the early evening, before the tide came high, setting their tackle straight, prepared for a bad night. Boards were up in houses down by the quay and in the low, flat parts of the village street. At the Ship Tavern, where we drink what is left to drink these days, I went with some friends and we talked about old times as you do when there are high storms and fine music in the wind; and we drank a good deal, sitting there in the long kitchen till near closing time; when suddenly everybody looked to the door which had swung wildly open.

'God bless my soul,' said an old fisherman, '' tes the first time in nigh thirty years I see Bob Starling come in here.'

I said nothing, but watched him. I was aware that I was drunk, in a sort of guarded drunkenness, prepared for anything, knowing this was the night I would get the story I wanted, and didn't want. He stood in the dark passage between the bar and the kitchen, and he asked, so quietly that it could hardly be heard, for a double whisky. Doubles aren't served now in this almost liquorless corner of England; he had to be content with a single. Drinking it at one nervous quick gulp he asked for another. I watched. He was a most extraordinary figure, in a long dirty leather jacket reaching nearly to his knees, his long thin legs in brown corduroy trousers much too short for him, which showed black woollen socks, full of holes, and made his feet seem huge. Over the leather jacket he had a mackintosh cape; on his head a yellow sou'wester cap tied under the chin, that gave his sharp ruddy face a babylike innocence. I thought he should be sitting in a pram dressed just as he was, sucking a dummy or playing with a rattle.

The second whisky went as quickly as the first. He asked for a third and was refused. He could have beer, he was told. But no, he didn't want beer. Out he went, with no sign of recognition to a soul, giving only a peering, darting look round the kitchen, as though he were looking for somebody; out he went and the door swung to and fro behind him, letting in a shivering snarl and twist from the wind.

Everybody started to chat about him. But suddenly, in my curiously alert condition, driven by the subconscious voice who commands most clearly under the stimulus of alcohol, I leapt up from my seat, snapped good night to my friends, and swung out of the door as though a pistol had shot me forward. Across the square, where the moon plunged from a continent of massed clouds, I could see him. He was going quickly up the cliff path, towards his own cottage, in that forward-leaning pensive walk of his, his great feet most oddly delicate, like a ballet dancer wearing enormous clogs. I got just behind him; then slackened my speed. He was muttering. 'The tide'll bring him back. It's a seventeen-foot tide, like it was then, and it'll throw him back, God help me.'

I nearly ran back to the Ship. I confess I was, for a few seconds, frightened. What had I stumbled upon? Leaning over the wall of the slipway I looked down to the harbour, which seemed to have come adrift in a churning mass of muddy sea. The night was roaring and howling, the wind playing havoc with slates and tiles and anything it could snatch. Dustbin lids clattered along the cobbled alleyways. Waiting there, gathering strength from the gale, I lost sight of old Starling. Had he gone up the Green Steps to his cottage? I didn't know. But suddenly I found my legs again and a new zest for life within me. When huge winds blow, either you must skulk with your face turned to the wall like a cornered rat; or else you must let the wind take you and blow you where it will. With enough liquor inside me, I felt suddenly mad, wild and very young. I had almost forgotten about old Starling. All I wanted to do was to soar up the cliff path like a rocket, charge round the corner, bellow some insult at the windows of a cottage where lived a rigid nonconformist family I disliked (and who disliked me), race recklessly up the dark slippery steps and find my way to the long slopes above the town and the harbour where you can watch the moon or the sun in a great expanse of sky. In short, if you like to put it more simply, I was flaming drunk and didn't care a damn what happened.

And so I went charging up the Green Steps, for the first (and only) time in my life not caring whether I stumbled and fell, only determined to get to the top and fill my lungs with wind.

I didn't get there as quickly as I had intended. Singing and shouting I don't know what, I stumbled half-way up, and nearly fell, reached out a hand to grab at something. My fingers closed round a door-knob. The door tottered open on weak hinges and I burst forward into a room dimly lit by a lamp with an untrimmed wick. I smelt the smoke of many years of oil-lamps. Bits of plaster dribbled down walls black with smoke. I was in old Starling's cottage, hurled into it, it seemed; and there he stood, his back to an inner door, his teeth chattering, the most abject picture of stark terror I had ever encountered.

I stared at him, he at me, and we didn't move for nearly a minute. Then he muttered in his thin cracked voice: 'You've come then. You've come to take your revenge.'

I was stark sober all at once. 'Who do you think I am?' I asked quietly.

'Him. Him I killed. A night like this too, when the wind got me and drove me to do it. You swore you'd come back, that was your last dying cry up the cliff when the – ' His words trailed away. (I was to notice how he had a habit of not finishing his sentences.)

'I'm not the man you killed – if you did kill a man. I'm your neighbour down the cliff. You know me. Look at me.'

I went a bit closer, turned up the spluttering lamp, and smiled at him in a forced sort of way. I didn't feel like smiling. I felt oddly angry. I felt it was a pity I wasn't 'him'; I felt he deserved what he so dreaded.

'You're not – you're not him – then why did you come up the steps like that, the way he always did, drunk and blind and mad after his nights down in the – and she, poor girl, having to keep a meal for him, keep him alive somehow, year in and year out, feeding a drunken maniac who had the insolence to think he could live as other people didn't because he could write poetry that – it's the highest tide for years and it was the night I killed him. He always said, his cry rang in my ears – but I've done the right thing, haven't I?'

He spoke in a disconnected, gasping way.

'I'm sure you've done the right thing,' I said, feeling none so sure. 'But look, couldn't you calm down? I'm not here to hurt you any way. I burst in by mistake. I admit I was drunk; but I'm sober as a judge now – '

'Not a judge, no, don't talk about a judge. I escaped. They wouldn't judge me. They wouldn't believe me.'

'Let's sit down and have a talk. I believe – '

'You shouldn't have come in here like that. It was a wicked thing to do, scaring me a night like this when the boats – as they did years ago and him trying to write poetry all the time, a maze of wild words he was, blood and bone and sun and moon raced in his veins, wild as a devil and greedy like a pig.'

He wouldn't move away from the door to the inner room.

'Tell me this,' I said very gently, 'are you talking about Robin Starling?'

'Yes, that's what he called himself and he was to be the great apocalyptic poet of the age, and because of that he could trample on everything and everybody and stamp up the Green

Steps back and down without thought for a soul. And Stella pouring out her love to him, always ready to take him back, whatever he did. I loved her too, but I never got her. Never.' He snapped his teeth and snarled on the word.

'Who was Robin Starling? Your brother?'

'Oh, closer than that, much closer. There are relationships, if you can understand, that are not defined in the books, closer than brother to brother, husband to wife, friend to friend, mother to child, much closer, so close that neither of us could breathe decent air. We lived here together, the three of us, him and me and Stella, and listen, what I shall tell you is the whole truth, what they won't believe, which is why I'm left alive to tell it now, because if they'd believed I'd have been hanged for it, justice they call that and − you don't believe me, do you, I can see you don't?'

'I believe every word you say. Please go on. I shan't tell anybody.'

'But I wish you to. I want everyone to know. When a man's committed a great crime the burden's too much to bear if nobody will believe he bears it. Will you tell them, will you tell the whole truth to help me bear it?'

'Yes, if you want me to, yes, I will.' (And this story began to be written from that moment.)

'But what *is* the truth?' I asked. 'You and him, this poet, Robin Starling, who was so close to you that − '

'All lived together and life was hell. For years I never spoke, never warned, only watched what was happening to him, the rot and the disease of his mind while he wasted his wonderful words on to paper at the price of other people's hearts. He wrote in the blood of others. And I watched him, never warning, never speaking. Silent all the time and in the evening − there was plenty to drink in those days, a man could get drunk on a few shillings, and Stella, she would have to sell things of her own, little bits of jewels given to her by her mother; she valued them, and paintings and books, they all had to go to get money for drink while I never said a word. Then I warned him; I said, if this doesn't stop I shall make it stop. He wouldn't listen. Sometimes in the grey morning light when he woke up all bleary and sick and parched in the throat with Stella beside him, then he would listen to me; and he'd agree, he'd say yes, he'd mend his ways, turn another direction, give up poetry and all the cheap tricks he'd turned his rotting mind to.

'In the mornings he'd admit to me that his fine spate of words meant nothing. He juggled words in a hat, like a conjuror; and people believed that what came out had the divine fire, but never had – a jingle, a prolonged nursery rhyme, that was all he was, aping all the raging poets who've ever dishonoured their manhood and left misery behind them. Yes, in the morning he'd see a little sense. But then, as time went on, he saw less and less; and even in the morning he'd drink, drink himself drunk again so that he could pour out more words. In there, behind me, I've got stacks of his writings, foolscap sheets with long lists of words on them and lines of poems he never finished. He never stopped; he was devoured by a fire.

'It wouldn't have mattered if it hadn't been for her. I couldn't stand by and watch her throw herself away; and other women he'd take when he wanted them, and always expect her to take him back as she always did. Then I got jealous, I wanted her for myself, I wanted to give her the things he couldn't give, a decent home and nice things like she longed to have from life. But she would never see me; never believed I had any independent existence . . . So it went on that way – years.'

There was a long pause. I still did not know what to make of the story. 'What did *you* do?' I mumbled. 'I mean – had you got work of your own?'

'Me? I was a shadow. *I was what was to be.* Didn't I tell you I was close to him, so close that I never left him for a second? I hadn't any work, only to watch him and trip him up; and he knew it all the time and would try to throttle me. Many a time he'd wake screaming, his hands round my throat, trying to shake the life out of me. Then she'd stop him somehow and I'd be safe again. It was him or me – don't you see – always him or me – one of us had to go. Well, he went.'

'Yes. You chased him up the cliff, didn't you – '

'Yes, yes – ' He spoke eagerly and came nearer to me. The door behind him blew open suddenly. In the dim light I could see masses of loose sheets of paper on the floor, and many books thrown down in a mass with fallen plaster and laths from the rotten roof. 'You know what happened then?'

'No. I was only told you chased him up the cliff.'

'Oh, more than that, much more. One night he came up the steps more drunk than usual, waking everybody, bellowing like a bull. Then I went mad, all reason left me. If he could sing and scream and bellow, so could I. If he had long black hair to scream in the wind, so had I. If he had nimble legs to leap like Pegasus up the Green Steps to the drying-ground, so had I. It went into me like poison into my blood, like a man suddenly charged with electricity – at the top, beyond the battery, where the cliff falls sheer down, there I got him. He was singing and swaying on the edge of the cliff as though he weren't subject to the rules of ordinary people. There was no thought about it. I had him round the waist in a second and over we both went in each other's arms, locked tight in mid-air. I don't know how it happened, but he wrestled with me in the air, and got free of me, and went hurtling to the bottom and – or did he, did he? That's what I never know. Did he float away like a lost angel? I never saw him. He'd gone and I clutched the cliff face and found a foothold and managed to cling there till they came with ropes to drag me up and – the Infirmary comes back to me now, I can see the ward where I lay, I was badly hurt and Stella came, every week she came to see me and said it would be all right, she'd always stay with me, always. But when I got back, and he'd gone for ever, and it was just the two of us, and I told her what I'd done, she only stared at me and called me Robin and said I'd never change for her, whatever happened. She wouldn't believe me, that I'd killed him. Nobody would listen – '

'I don't understand this. Somebody must have known he'd gone? There must have been an inquest or – '

'Nothing, nothing. Don't you understand the frightfulness

of it? They all said *I* was him. You see, we were so close, we were so alike, we exactly resembled one another. All the time the three of us lived here, even Stella never noticed me, never tried to draw me out from my silences. Only when he and I were quite alone could I talk to him and him to me. Then, when I'd killed him and came back, she thought I was him, and nothing – until I started to get work and earn a living which he'd never done; and one day some editor wrote and said he wanted to print some of his poems and I wrote back and said that Robin Starling had fallen over the cliff and was dead and that I was his brother and dealing with his affairs. Then Stella began to behave strangely. She said I was mad, that the fall had affected my brain, and that I ought to have medical treatment and – I worked, so hard I worked, and I saw my life's ambition before me and knew I'd achieve it. But not her; I couldn't win her. She left me and never came back.'

'Your life's ambition? What was that?'

In a corner, by the grate where dead ashes lay with charred paper, was his long stiff broom. Pointing to it, 'That,' he said. 'I knew I'd have to come to it. Each man must fulfil his destiny, you see; that's how it works. It was prophesied for me, by him, and it's come true as I knew it must come true. And now – now, though I dread it, I want him back. I want to hear him sing again as he used to, I want to watch his legs flying up the Green Steps to the hill-sides he loved, and I want to follow him. When he comes back, I'll follow him, yes, I'll follow him, in a great wind when the tide's high he'll come back as he said he would and then – ' He muttered away into himself and I could no longer hear the words.

The wind gave a sudden charge at the house and papers rustled along the floor in the darkened inner room. I thought of the wild and happy parties that must have taken place here years ago. I saw the old scavenger bending down to pick up a sheet of yellowed paper. 'His,' he muttered. 'His words. All meaningless. All meaningless.'

He handed the paper to me and turned his back. Taking a poker he toyed the ashes with it, then crouched on a chair,

holding his long hands out to no spark of warmth. Above him
on the wall was a great patch of dampness, furry and mildewed,
like a map of some fabulous country. Suddenly I knew that I
hadn't a word of consolation to give and I turned back to the
door, feeling desperately miserable. I wished I had been 'him',
that slain self who so tormented him.

At the door, 'I know he'll come back to you one day,' I said;
and felt that it was true.

Then I went outside, closed the door, and walked inch
by inch up the slippery steps to the hill-side where the pure
moon had soared through a gap in the black clouds. The wind
was easing off a little. The night was fresh and the salt of the
sea strong in my nostrils. I read the lines on the bit of paper
he'd given me.

> 'Landlocked in this sandpride of westfallen moonflowers
> I (in my archery) to you before wisdom its windows
> Swings follywards, turn with the splint of the stinging finger.'

It made no sense, but it was strangely contemporary. I could
see by the freshness of the ink that it had only recently been
written. But the writing was of an old man.

He is still living, still the village scavenger, and never a word
have I had with him from that day, and never shall I. I am tormented whenever I see him; and yet there is a strange feeling of certainty within me about him, as though I knew that
he would find the way up the steps and follow, as he wished
to follow, that once-hated, bitterly-resented truer self of his
whom he killed years ago. When I see him I know that because
of the great division in him the great union is already achieved.
He is a poet who has had to work out fatally in his own nature
the disintegration of our times. Like the Poet, the Scavenger is
lifted outside the laws of men. One by one his own words go
into the dust-cart to be burnt in the waste land behind the village. The smoke of those words rises and drifts over the roofs
to the sea. And the lines that he wrote which moved me as a
boy prophesy for him the destiny he desires.

II

My Lady Sweet, Arise

Miss Polly Ponsonby lived in a small yellow-bricked cottage in Baker's Lane, a narrow, wooded, little hill winding down by the side of a recreation park in Sydenham. It had been her father's house, and after his death, just before the war, she had inherited it. He had been a chiropodist who, in his spare time, played the flute, Polly accompanying him on the piano. They had always been very fond of music, a fact which Mrs Ponsonby, who had died when Polly was a girl of ten, had resented. For she had had no ear for music and was tormented daily when Polly began to learn the violin, then to take singing lessons from Dr Murdoch, the organist at the parish church. Mrs Ponsonby had no use for that sort of thing. Polly and her father were secretly happier when she passed away, leaving them to hours of peaceful music-making on long winter nights after Mr Ponsonby returned from his consulting room in Sydenham High Street.

After Mr Ponsonby's death, Polly, then aged forty-seven, decided it was wrong to live alone. So she took lodgers, usually young men or women who had business in the City and were out all day.

One of these lodgers, Barley Merton, an actress working in repertory at the Sydenham Hippodrome, became a close friend of Polly's. She was 'such a lady,' often talking of her family in the country, and her young brother Ryland (known as 'Rye') who did something very important in the West End – Polly never knew what. And Barley liked old Polly, so there was a pleasant friendly atmosphere in the cottage.

Polly was a grotesque to look at. There could be no two opinions as to that. She knew it herself. A pink and very wrinkled face, a mass of thin grey hair, a small, stout body, and abnormally large flat feet (which her father had ignored, for he had always refused to bring his professional skill to the service of his family – a defect in an otherwise excellent man) these were presented to the world in clothes which looked as though they were the spoils of a succession of jumble-sales. Moreover, she never seemed to be able to dress for the time of year. In summer she might suddenly dig out an old grey fox fur and a check tweed overcoat hanging like a sack round her lumpy figure; in winter she might venture to the park wearing a flowered cotton frock and a floppy straw hat.

'Really, Miss Ponsonby, you take the giddy biscuit,' Barley said one evening, sipping her Ovaltine on her return from the theatre. 'Who but you would think of sporting white silk gloves on the foulest December day?'

Polly smiled. When she smiled her eyes – small and dark brown – seemed to disappear. Barley often wondered how one knew that Miss Ponsonby was smiling. But there couldn't be any mistake about it.

'It's the artist in me.' Polly spoke with quiet modesty. 'Mr Ponsonby was just the same. I really don't notice trivial things like weather, dear. I think clothes are there to serve our impulses. When I got up this morning, goody-goody! I said, white silk gloves today, my lady. Surely you, Miss Merton, being such an artist yourself, understand the *call*?'

Barley, whose impulses led to an excessive number of honey-coloured curls, and who had a way of pirouetting through puddles in very high heels, nodded thoughtfully. 'Of course, people of a certain class can do what they like and it's always right. Dad, for example, eats peas with a spoon – just to show that he hasn't any use for all this gentility humbug. You and me are much of a muchness, Miss Ponsonby.'

'Except, my dear, in the matter of looks,' Polly murmured sadly.

'Oh, what are looks? Of course, in my profession, they *do* count, you can't get away from that. But in your case – ' Barley stopped suddenly, feeling she might hurt Miss Ponsonby.

'What were you going to say, dear?'

'Well, to tell you God's truth, I was thinking of that performance of *Hiawatha* by the Sydenham Choral Society you gave me a ticket for. Funny pack of guys, aren't they? But mind you, they *can* sing, that's what matters.'

'I think, dear Miss Merton, that musicians, developing as they do so acutely the sense of *sound,* often possess a very vague sense of sight. I expect that is why I look so garish myself – and I do, of course, I know I do. But there we are. *You* are meant to be seen – and *I* am meant to be heard.'

'Well, I shouldn't get far if they couldn't hear me.'

'Of course, my dear. But a pretty face and a pleasing figure is what chiefly matters on the stage. And you do not go to a musical performance to look at the performers; you go to listen.'

'Well, it takes all sorts, as they say. Human beings are funnier than apes. If I didn't think so, I'd go crackers. If it weren't for my brother Rye sending me nylons every so often, and some decent chocolates, and you looking after me as you do here, I think I'd chuck everything up.'

'Oh, but why, dear, why? You're *so* brilliant.'

'Not me. A lousy actress, stuck in a bloody rep in this backwater.'

'I have never regarded Sydenham as a backwater.'

'Oh well, you were born and bred here. And music's different somehow. You float away on it and forget yourself. Same with me when I'm actually on. Every time I get my call I feel as though I'm sprouting a pair of wings.'

Miss Ponsonby was suddenly silent. Barley thought that a rich blush had suffused her wrinkled features.

'If you know what I mean,' she continued. 'You know that thing you sing sometimes – "O for the wings of a dove?" Don't you ever feel like that? When I go on the stage I feel as though I never want to come off, whatever part I'm playing. It's easier on the stage.' Still Miss Ponsonby was silent.

When Barley went up to bed presently she heard the sound of the violin downstairs. Miss Ponsonby was playing 'Hark,

hark the lark'. She played it over and over again, and then tried it on the piano, singing it in her pure and limpid boy-like voice. It touched Barley. But after a time she got tired of it. 'Why can't the old geezer go to bed?' she muttered, turning over and over and trying to blot out the sound by burying her face in the pillow.

Not long after this, Polly took to going to the Spiritualist Church at the bottom end of Baker's Lane. Although she had for years been a communicant at the parish church, she had often admitted to Barley that the services never quite gave her the satisfaction she needed. Then it came out, in conversation, that shortly before the end of his life, Mr Ponsonby had also fallen for spiritualism. This was because he had dreamt one night that a client with six toes on one foot (two of them permanently crossed) would call upon him; and the next day it had happened. Old Ponsonby had never been quite the same man after that. 'There are more things in Heaven and earth' he had muttered over his evening baked-beans-on-toast; and a few days later had ambled self-consciously off to the little red-brick building, with the green slate roof, which he had previously so despised.

Polly would never accompany him to this haunt of spirit-rappers, and always shied off the subject whenever he brought it up. He stopped going to Church to the dismay of the vicar, for Mr Ponsonby had been a sidesman, and would occasionally consent to sing in the choir if the anthem had a suitable solo for him. It caused an unhappy rift between Polly and her father; but she never attempted to make him change his mind, neither did he seek to convert her to his new religion. Only once, after the first delicate arguments, did he refer to whatever it was that went on down the lane. (It was always referred to as 'Down the Lane'.) That was when he said, casually, one rainy night on his return:

'Your mother spoke tonight.'

Polly had naturally been startled, even scared. But she hid this. 'What did she say?' she asked.

Mr Ponsonby thought a long time before replying. Then, 'Only, that there was no dratted music where she'd gone.'

He looked at his wife's picture on the sideboard. It stood in an intricately carved silver frame and showed Amelia Ponsonby in the full richness of womanhood, aged thirty-five, with large silky eyelashes, a mount of hair like a finely turned loaf, and a generous bosom which Mr Ponsonby dreamt of more frequently than his daughter could have guessed. It was the one thing he had really liked about his wife.

'I'm not sure,' he had said after studying her picture for a long time, 'that your mother wasn't right to hate music. It gets you nowhere.'

This had made Polly flush with anger. 'On the contrary, it gets you everywhere,' she snapped. 'And I didn't think I'd live to hear you say such things, Father. Spiritualism has ruined you.'

It had been a painful moment. Never was the subject mentioned again, and Mr Ponsonby went less frequently down the lane, spending more of his time in the Talma Tavern where he would play darts. Musical evenings became rare, to Polly's great sorrow.

That was all many years ago. The war had passed since then, bringing severe tests of Polly's Faith. She had continued to go to Church, to sing and play the piano and the violin, sometimes with a friend or two in the Choral Society, more often alone. Flying bombs only brought out an inherent courage in her. Nothing would make *her* move to the country, she said. If God meant her to die here, let Him take her in His own way. She even got rather doggedly fond of the 'doodlebugs' after the first week or so. At least, she said, they were in good company with the fowls of the air; she didn't mean this, but it gave her strength to carry on.

She never quite knew why she suddenly, and so long after, fell for her father's religion; but it had certainly grown upon her after the talk with Barley, when she had played 'Hark, hark the lark' downstairs in the gaslight while Barley tried to sleep. For several days following this talk, she would find herself repeating, in her mind, over and over again the alluring phrase: *My lady sweet, arise.*

And then one day, she did a thing she rarely did; she looked in a mirror. Good Heavens! How plain she was! Far plainer than even she had supposed. It dawned upon her that her mother must have resented this atrociously plain, even ugly little girl; for Mrs Ponsonby had had the flaunting majesty of a gipsy and the lips of a courtesan.

'Oh dear, how very ugly,' sighed Polly.

And then, in order to comfort herself, began to sing. There was no doubt about that, anyway. The sound that issued from those dry thin lips was divinely beautiful; and she knew it. If only, she thought, I could give *one* concert. At the Wigmore Hall. Or even one of the Sunday night concerts at the Capitol Cinema in Sydenham. But it would never do. With a face like that she could never go before the public. All that Barley had said about the ugliness of the singers in the Choral Society came back to her. It was true. A hideous lot. But the compensations were great.

Going round with the vacuum cleaner, she sang all the time. Once, lifting a chair away from the crowded carpet, she felt a strange little pain in her breast as she touched a high note. She was not singing any known melody; but carolling spontaneously, without words and sometimes indulging, with an impious sense of abandon, in a trill. She had to stop and sit on the sofa and clutch a cushion, the pain in her breast was so acute. It seemed to grow worse when she was not singing; and yet to sing any more was an effort. Forcing herself to do so, she commenced to warble fitfully. The pain left her. For the rest of the morning, as she went about her housework, she sang the whole time.

When Barley came home she said she thought Polly looked very pale.

'Oh, it's nothing my dear. I had a strenuous day. Such long queues at the greengrocer's and the butcher's. Have your tea now, while it's hot. I wish that you'd been with me to-day, dear. I caused quite a sensation in the street.'

'In the street?' Barley stared. 'What've you been up to?'

'I started to sing while I was waiting in a queue outside Hobson's, the butcher's.'

'What? Sing? Did you send round the hat?'

Miss Ponsonby took this seriously, and looked a little hurt.

'I've no need for *that,* my dear. Mr Ponsonby left me well provided for.'

'I was only joking.' Barley wolfed toasted cheese furiously. 'But what do you mean, you started to sing?'

'Just what I say. People looked so surprised, but rather pleased, I thought. I think it meant something to them, as it did to me.'

'I should think it darn well did. What did you sing?'

'Oh, anything that came to me. "Bid me discourse," "Where the bee sucks," snatches from Puccini – just anything. It didn't matter.'

Barley paused with a forkful of toasted cheese. Then she asked: 'Did you sing that one you're always singing – what is it – something about the lark?'

'No. No. I didn't do that one.'

'Just why did you do it, Miss Ponsonby?'

'Well, Barley – might I call you Barley? It's such a sweet name – and will you call me Polly?'

'Righty-oh. Well, why did you do it, Polly?'

'I had a bad pain here,' she vaguely flicked a long finger towards her flat chest, 'it bothered me all the early part of the morning. But I noticed that when I sang, it left me. Goody-goody, I said, this puts me right. There's no doubt about it: music does keep you going.'

'Did you sing right out loud?'

'I never do sing loud, dear. I haven't that sort of voice. Listen.'

She started to sing.

Later that night Barley wrote to her brother.

Dear old Rye,

I'm a bit worried. I believe the old girl I lodge with is going off her nut. You remember I told you she went spooky some weeks ago and started dabbling in spiritualism? Now she can't stop singing. She's warbling away like mad as I write this and it kind of gets into me and scares me a bit. Wish you'd come down this weekend and tell me what you think of her. She says she's got a pain and when she sings it stops. She's awful sweet, you know, though as shapeless as last year's Christmas pudding; and she couldn't have been kinder to me. She's just gone to the kitchen with the supper remains and I can hear her on a high note. Now she's trilling like a penny whistle. It doesn't sound like ordinary singing. Do you remember that Chaplin film years ago when he swallowed a kid's whistle and every time he tried to speak it shrilled out a high note? It's rather like that. I – '

Barley put down her pen suddenly. The sound was getting on her nerves. She went to the kitchen, carrying the cheese dish through. Polly was standing on tip-toe before the sink, washing dishes, and still singing. As Barley watched her, she put aside the washing-up mop and held on to the sink with both her hands. From her open lips flooded an arabesque of pellucid sound, pure and spontaneous. There were no words. One of her feet left the ground; the other still stretched on tip-toe. It was a bewildering and grotesque scene.

'Polly!' cried Barley, 'what's the matter with you?'

She turned round. Still singing, she held her fingers to her lips as though to ask for silence. Then she suddenly collapsed and fell to the floor. Barley got her to a chair, dabbed water on her forehead, managed presently to revive her, then fled out to ring for a doctor.

The doctor said there was nothing whatever wrong with her. But she still complained of the nagging pain in her breast. He suggested an X-ray examination. A week later she went to the hospital and submitted to this. While she waited, she began to sing, startling the staff and delighting patients in distant wards. It was a truly Heavenly sound, far more flute-like than it should have been. She did not seem able to stop herself. They could find nothing irregular which could have caused the pain. Pure nervous imagination, it was said. The doctor suggested a long rest in a nursing-home. But she said she would rather not go. Her singing might only disturb the other inmates.

So she returned home. Barley began to wonder whether she ought to look for other lodgings. By now, it was common gossip that Miss Ponsonby had gone strange. Often, on her return from the theatre, Barley would find a group of boys and girls gathered outside the park gates, opposite the cottage, listening to Polly and giggling and making rude remarks while she stood in the open doorway, filling the night with luscious liquid musical sequences, sometimes slithering away in Ravel-like phrases of tender and evocative lyricism, sometimes just staying for a long time on one trilling note, then falling, then rising. She would stand with her hands clutching the door knob, as though she feared to have another collapse.

The crowds would get bigger. With closing time at the Talma semi-drunks would wander down Baker's Lane to hear the old girl going at it. It grew intolerable for Barley. Yet she felt she could never desert one who had been so kind to her, giving her hot-waterbottles in winter, always bringing up a tray of tea and toast to the snug little bedroom which over-looked the gentle slopes of the wooded park, and bearing most patiently with Barley's little outbursts of temperament.

In desperation, one hot summer night, when Polly was singing over the grey phloxes in the small square garden, Barley wrote again to her brother.

For God's sake come down and help me. I'm afraid she'll get locked up or something. Nobody cares. It's just a local joke. Those damned spiritualists have deserted her. She hardly ever talks now. It's music all the time and it's driving me bats. But I can't help loving the old thing.

And I forgot to tell you – something very funny's happening. She's growing *smaller*.

When Rye got this letter he decided to investigate. He had just joined forces with a chap who ran a Mammoth Fair, touring all over the country. Freaks were rare nowadays. This sounded the goods.

Rye was thirty, looked forty and behaved twenty. He wore a pale fawn teddybear coat, a startling silk scarf, a wide-brimmed stetson hat and carried a black cane. His hair was black and was arrowed devilishly over his eyes. There was a flash of diamonds about him; and he was always bringing illicit treasures from the large secret pockets of his coat. Cigars, half bottles of spirits, perfume, silk stockings, peaches, tickets for boxing matches, silver pencils, chocolate liqueurs – Barley had long ceased to register any surprise at what emerged from these prodigious pockets.

Polly didn't like him at first. He was common, you could tell after a glance. And she had always understood that Barley's brother had gone to Lancing College and on to Cambridge and later into business of some sort. 'There's nothing Rye hasn't done,' Barley had said. 'He's a wiz of the wizards.'

But after a few minutes, Polly warmed to his breezy style, his slap-on-the-thigh manner, his way of treating inanimate objects as though they were close personal friends.

It was his remarks about Mr Ponsonby's flute that won her. This stood, in its case, which was open, on top of the piano. It was never touched, except to be dusted, and every Saturday a bowl of fresh flowers was put before it. When Rye came the flowers were cherry-pie and scarlet salvias, an exotic display in a crystal bowl. It caught his eye at once.

'I say,' he said, 'jolly fine instrument you've got there. Must be worth a packet. Can I take it out?'

'I'd prefer that you didn't, Mr Merton. It was my father's dearest possession.'

'Quite understand! Handsome little place you've got, Miss

Ponsonby.' He sat down and stroked the back of a mahogany musical box, a small treasure which stood on a three-legged bamboo table in the window with the ferns and potted fuchsias.

'Now I'll get you tea, Mr Merton.' She rose rather weakly. Yes, thought Rye, there was no doubt about it; she certainly looked strange. And very shrunken.

'Don't you worry, Polly,' said Barley. 'I'll get the tea while you and Rye have a chat.'

She opened her mouth. Barley knew the signs and left for the kitchen hurriedly. But Polly didn't sing. Instead:

'Let me be quite frank, Mr Merton. Why have you come to see me?'

Running a chubby forefinger over the mouse-coloured velvet of the Prince Consort easy-chair in which he sat, 'Why not, Miss Ponsonby? You've been a saint to Barley. She's always telling me how good you are. By the way, I've got something you might like. Accept it as a little present.' He snapped out from his breast pocket, a very pretty piece of costume jewellery: a small brooch of paste diamonds, shaped like a soprano clef, and mounted on five gold bars. 'Know you're fond of music,' he said, 'and happened to pick this up and thought – well, there you are!'

She was charmed. She blushed. She had not been given any such present for a very long time.

'Oh, Mr Merton!' She pinned it to her dress and thanked him warmly. 'Yes, it's a very happy choice for me. Music is my whole life. I expect Barley has told you.'

'She mentioned how keen you were on singing.'

'Yes. I do sing a great deal.' Again, a pause, and she half opened her mouth. Rye waited. He thought it was about time she started.

But she seemed determined not to sing that afternoon. 'I want to ask you something,' she said, 'as a man of the world, Mr Merton.'

'Carry right on and no charge.'

She appeared to have difficulty in speaking; an agonized

look darkened her face. 'Only this,' she said. 'I want to know Mr Merton: is there any *law* against singing in the street – or in any public place? Is it illegal?'

He slapped his knee and leant across towards her.

'Now that's queer,' he said, 'For that's just what I wanted to talk about. I might as well be frank, too. Barley's worried about you. She thinks there'll be trouble about your singing. Mind you – she and I, and people who *know* – people who understand the artistic impulse and so on, we *like* it. At least, I haven't heard it. But I'm pretty certain I should like it.'

'Wait till you get it all night,' muttered Barley, who was listening in the passage while the kettle boiled.

'You see, Mr Merton, I *have* to sing. But lately I've grown conscious of strange looks from people in the street. I'm afraid, oh dear! I'm afraid they don't really care for it as I do and Barley does. And I never feel myself unless I'm singing.'

'Why should you? I mean, why shouldn't you? But the trouble is, Miss Ponsonby, we're living in a world that's hot against anything they call eccentric. If I had my way I'd let you sing all day and night. But it's no use denying it; sooner or later, if you go on warbling in the market place, they'll put you under lock and key.'

'Oh no, oh no,' she whispered.

'Yes, oh yes. What I want to say is – sing when you're at home, as much as you like. Nobody can object to that. But try to curb the impulse when you're out and about.'

'To be locked up – oh dear! In a *cage,* perhaps, oh how dreadful!'

'Cage? What makes you say cage?' He looked at her quickly. The word linked up with his own thoughts.

'Linnets, Mr Merton. You know what they do to linnets?'

Her voice had sunk away to a scratched needly sound, like an old record on an old gramophone. And her face was pale and ashen. Rye began to feel worried. He could see his bird slipping through his fingers. And he thought it was about time she treated him to a song.

'You mustn't get downhearted, Miss Ponsonby,' he said

cheerfully. 'Stick to it when stuck. That's our family motto.
It's always served me well. As I see it, you're stuck away here in
Sydenham, wasting a wonderful gift. Has it ever occurred to
you? Beat the world, before it beats you.'

'What – do – you – mean?'

She looked scared. And even as he watched her, she seemed
to shrink into her chair. There didn't seem to be any shape to
her. Only her large flat feet, which kept shifting on the worn
carpet, had retained any life.

'I mean,' said Rye, 'that it's up to you not to let folk think
you're barmy – that's straight from the shoulder, my dear lady,
and I speak as a friend. I look at it this way. If you've got an
exceptional gift for anything, unless you use it, unless you
market it to the best possible advantage, the world'll merely
say you're crackers and put you away where you don't want
to go. All musical geniuses are bats, if you look at them from
ordinary standpoints. Look at friend Mozart. Do you call him
human? Thumping out the jolly old semiquavers at the age
of four. If the authorities had had their way, bang would have
gone Wolfgang into a looney bin. Fortunately he had a father
who knew his job. What did that father do? Marketed the kid
promptly. Romped him round Europe to all the courts. Result
– world cries genius!'

He sank his voice to a tense whisper. She was staring at him.
There was a tiny point of burning light in her small, dark eyes.
'That's what somebody's got to do for you – before it's too late.
In other words – here I am, and I'm your devoted from now
on. We'll go fifty-fifty. I don't want more than my share. And I
can promise you the time of your life, and every comfort. And
you can warble in eighteen different keys at once. How about
it?'

'About what? I don't understand.'

'The show business, Miss Ponsonby. Easy money and no
more persecution from neighbours!'

'The *show* business? You mean – '

'I mean – money, a friend of mine runs a travelling joint –
what some people call a Fair but what I prefer to call a – '

She suddenly gave a pathetic little shriek. At that moment Barley entered with the tea.

'Oh no, no,' cried Polly. Her words seemed to torture her. The veins in her throat bulged. Her tiny nose twitched and her fingers fumbled clumsily at her dress. 'How dreadful – how dreadful of you!' Stumbling out of the room she went upstairs. They heard her lock the door of her bedroom.

'Now you've dished it,' said Barley.

'Not on your life. She'll come round to the idea. But, blast me, I wish the old eagle would pipe up a bit. I've only got your word that she can sing at all.'

Not a sound came from upstairs. Barley went up, tried the door, knocked, begged Polly to let her in. Not a sound. Going down, the brother and sister sipped cups of tea and crumbled some of Polly's seed-cake on their blue-ringed plates.

'I'm horribly worried, Rye,' said Barley. 'I didn't have time to tell you. This morning old Mrs Jackson who lives opposite said to me that everybody agreed it would be kinder to send her away somewhere. They get tired of the crowds round here, you see. But she's not dotty, I'm quite sure she's not.'

'You wait. I'll catch her. We'll make a pile out of this, old dear.'

'Oh, Rye, it doesn't seem fair.'

'Why not? If it's going to save her from a padded cell?'

But he never did catch her. All the rest of that evening no sound at all came from upstairs. About nine, Rye got tired of waiting and went round to the Talma for a quick one. Chatting there to some of the regulars, old Sydenham folk who had known Polly's father and always had great respect for Polly herself, what Barley had feared was confirmed by them. They all spoke sadly of her, as though it were only a matter of days before she would have to be put away. 'But why – why?' argued Rye angrily, thumping his fist on the counter. 'What the devil's wrong with the old lady?'

'It ain't right nor proper,' said one, 'for a lady to go on singing in the street. It upsets people, for one thing. And it ain't human, not that sound, not human at all.'

More and more he longed to hear her sing. But when he went back to the cottage, she was still upstairs, and not a single note had escaped from her lips since his absence.

Gloomily, Rye picked up the precious family flute and lingered the pistons. 'I've offended her, that's what it is,' he said. 'Curse myself for being so impatient. I should have got her to sing first, then, bit by bit, worked the idea into her head. I know she'd be happy once she was on the road with the gang. There's a bearded female who's an absolute duck. She and Polly would chum up in no time. It's only because she's got false ideas of what's respectable. You'll have to bring her to it, Barley. Otherwise she's for it.'

'Not if she goes on like this,' said Barley, 'silent as night up there. It frightens me, Rye. I kind of feel I don't like being left alone with her any more.'

'Well, I've got to be back to-night, old dear. Business in Petticoat Lane at crack of dawn. Wire me if anything begins to happen. I'll be down like a shot.'

He put the mouthpiece of the flute to his lips and tried to blow a note from it. 'Might encourage her,' he said.

But he couldn't get a sound from it, however hard he tried. Screwing his lips to a thin crack, he went redder in the face, blowing for all his might.

Suddenly a door upstairs was hurled open, there were stumbling footsteps down the stairs, and Polly burst into the room, her eyes inflamed with tears. In a choking voice she addressed Rye.

'Put that flute down, Mr Merton. Leave my house at once. You have come here with an intolerable proposition. I have made up my mind. I will never sing again. Never!'

He tried to pacify her, but to no avail. Barley got her to a chair and soothed her. 'I've nothing against you, my dear,' she muttered. 'But I cannot have your brother here. I beg you to ask him to leave. I know he meant well. But he has killed my purest impulse.'

She would not look at him. When he had gone, for half the night she sat in the sitting room, staring at the ferns in the window, and once or twice taking up her mother's photograph. 'You've won, you've won,' Barley heard her saying.

True to her own words, she did not sing again — for several weeks.

During the next few weeks Polly was diligent in offering her lodger all the comforts she had been accustomed to. But day by day she seemed to grow thinner till she was no more than a shapeless bag of flesh and bone. Barley took to being out more often than she need have been. It was too much for her. She almost longed for her to sing again. She would have preferred the crowds and the talk of the neighbours to this gloomy and resigned silence.

Then, one day, something happened to restore a faint gleam of life to poor Polly Ponsonby. An old friend, who had kept away for some weeks, not knowing how to approach Polly during her eccentric period, came again to see her. This friend was one of the oldest members of the Choral Society to which Polly also belonged. It was a Society with a long tradition of fine choral singing, some of the older members having been in the Handel Festival Choir. And they had just been invited, by the management of the Albert Hall, to supply the vocal parts in a Delius concert which was to be given in October. The work for which voices were needed was *Appalachia*. It was unfamiliar to Polly. But her friend arrived with the score, picked out the treble line on the piano, and begged her to join them.

'It will be so good for you,' she said, 'and take you out of yourself, Polly dear.' She patted her affectionately. In the past the two ladies had often sung together.

Polly consented. And thereafter, daily grew more excited at the prospect of singing in the Albert Hall. Rehearsals began in a day or so, under their own local conductor, at the Town Hall, Polly went along hardly aware of the others, who whispered about her, and waited tensely for her to open her mouth. The conductor, Dr Murdoch, shook her warmly by the hand. He was an old man and had known her for years, having been her first singing master. It had distressed him that she had lately become the victim of such a curious scandal; but he, like many other friends, had never quite had the courage to go and talk to her during the time of her flute-like fluency. It had been too embarrassing.

'Stinking old sods,' said Barley to Rye. 'They all deserted her; now they're all fawning on her again, waiting for her to start singing. Makes you sick.'

It was rather a loose judgement. For most of her friends had been acutely sorry for her, but too bewildered by what had become a major sensation to be able to talk with her on the old terms.

Still, here she was now, back with her friends, and nobody was gladder than Dr Murdoch, who had always had a high appreciation of her musical abilities. The Delius was not a very easy work for these amateur singers. It would need considerable rehearsal before they went to London to rehearse with the orchestra. Dr Murdoch was therefore delighted to see Polly in her old place again, with the first trebles; and he prayed that she might not take it into her head to sing in the extraordinary manner which had provoked so much talk in the neighbourhood, and beyond.

This did not happen – to the disappointment of the sensationalists. What did happen was stranger – though only detected by those who sat near to Polly, including her old friend Miss Dunstable, the librarian. Although, at that first, and at subsequent rehearsals, Polly opened her mouth and appeared to be singing, she never actually made a sound. Miss Dunstable listened carefully. No – not even a whisper. That limpid treble of Polly's seemed to have vanished like a dried-up spring. Miss Dunstable, being tactful, said no word to anyone. Dr Murdoch, with even his keen ear, was unable to detect, amongst a choir of nearly a hundred men and women, that one of them was contributing precisely nothing. Only Miss Dunstable and another lady, Mrs Reeks, a chemist's wife, realised what was happening, or rather, what was not happening. Yet Polly herself seemed to be completely satisfied. She even remarked, at the end of the first rehearsal: 'How lovely it is to sing again, Lorna! And what a beautiful work it is!'

Lorna Dunstable glanced significantly at Brenda Reeks.

'Yes, dear,' she said. 'One can see how you enjoy it.'

At the next rehearsal – the same thing happened. At the third – again, not a sound from that wrinkled little face.

Barley knew nothing of all this. Like anyone else, she was merely happy to see Polly so much more like her old self – her pre-flute self. And on the day of the concert she helped Polly put the finishing touches to the white satin dress she would have to wear. It was hard not to laugh at her appearance; and Barley felt glad that her work at the theatre would not allow her to be present at the concert. To watch all those mummies warbling away would have been, Barley knew, too much for her. But she reminded Rye and advised him to be present, in case of anything unusual happening.

What happened at that concert was very unusual indeed. And yet it was not detected by even Rye Merton, who had taken a seat fairly near the orchestra and was able to pick out Miss Ponsonby, in her white dress, with all the other ladies – young, middle-aged, old, thin, fat, red-faced, white-faced, cross-eyed, bandy-legged – who filled the tiered seats behind the orchestra. He could pick out Polly, chiefly because she was so small, standing at least a foot and a half below Lorna Dunstable and Brenda Reeks. (Brenda was an Olympic woman of operatic build; Lorna was sylph-like, and swayed like a murmuring reed when she sang.) In between these two, Polly looked like a faint white blob, a large piece of cottonwool dropped there by mistake.

Rye watched her eagerly. It seemed literally hours before the chorus had anything to do. Delius, an impractical composer, seems to take a delight in dragging on an enormous chorus and only using it for the last few episodes of an abnormally long and luscious work. Rye was terribly bored. He was no musician and kept glancing at the programme notes, trying to make out which variation they had reached. They all seemed much the same to him, except that some were loud, some soft, some slow, some fast.

After hours of this, Rye began to get restless and long for the bar. The chorus hadn't even stood up yet. Perhaps, thought Rye, he had made a mistake and they were singing in the next work. But there was an interval after the *Appalachian Variations*. No; sooner or later all these grotesque women in white and these waxwork dummies in black would open their mouths.

Sure enough they did. The men first, singing la-la-la in soft undertones of sound, like waves on a seashore. Then more la-la-la. Then much more from the orchestra and Rye began to think the women were only brought there just to fill up the seats. He had, by now, lost interest in Polly, though he noticed her from time to time. Her face was always turned to the conductor.

Then, at long last, with a wave of the hand from the conductor, all the ladies and gentlemen of Sydenham Choral Society rose to their feet. One could almost hear their sigh of relief. And now, everybody's eye was fixed on Sir Kenneth Corporal who, sleek and black-haired, with a wasp-like waist and delicate engraving fingers with which he seemed to describe the shape of music in the air – suddenly poised his baton towards the singers. A glorious sound of music burst forth. Lorna and Brenda leant forward, giving of their utmost. Their great moment had come. The orchestra was silent while the singers poured out Delius's exotic and vigorous harmonies.

Heigh-ho, heigh-ho, down the mighty river
Aye, Honey, I'll be gone when next the whippoorwill's a-calling . . .

And then the baritone soloist (distinguished from the common hacks of Sydenham, by full evening dress with tails and white tie): 'And don't you be too lonesome, love, and don't you fret and cry.'

It was during this snatch of solo that Rye Merton noticed, far up in the glass dome of the hall, a tiny dark speck. It did not impress itself on him greatly. But when he next looked along the first row of the lady trebles, he realized that there was a space where Miss Ponsonby had been.

Neither Brenda nor Lorna, her immediate neighbours in the hall, had anything to report in the inquiries which followed. They had been so intent on the singing, their eyes so glued to Sir Kenneth (who had been a bit of a martinet at the morning's rehearsal), that all thought of anything but the music had gone, as it should have gone, right out of their minds. It was not, in fact, until the work ended on the long drawn-out string notes, that Lorna realized the place next to her was empty. And that, during the singing, with the women's first entry, she thought she had heard a faint chirruping sound. Brenda said that she had definitely felt something soft and light flutter against her cheek, for only a second. Other strange stories bewildered the curious. Sir Kenneth said that he had been put off his beat, for a moment or two, by the sudden intrusion of a peculiarly beautiful singing, far above him. He had glanced up but seen nothing.

Mr Henry Brissey, the soloist, came forward with an astonishing yarn. He had never noticed Miss Ponsonby at all. She would be to him, only one of many undistinguished ladies. But he had noticed, he said, a small dark bird, flutter away from the front row of the trebles and disappear quickly far up into the roof of the hall.

He was, naturally, laughed at. But nobody had anything more plausible to report. Miss Polly Ponsonby, who had certainly taken her place with the other ladies at the beginning of the concert, had completely disappeared by the end of the first half.

After endless investigations by the police, it was finally assumed that Miss Ponsonby must be dead. In her will she left the house, all its contents, and her small bank balance to Barley, 'in return for companionship through a great crisis'. There was a legacy of a hundred pounds for a Bird-watching Society. One curious feature of the will related to Mr Ponsonby's flute: this was to be given, if possible, Christian burial. Barley buried it herself, reverently, with Rye in attendance, in the back-garden, and made a little bed of forget-me-nots over it.

It was many weeks before Barley realized a curious thing. Always, outside the house, vaguely in the air, there seemed to be the distant and heavenly sound of a bird singing. This persisted, sometimes far away, sometimes near, throughout the winter months. Spring came. There were days when Barley thought she could see the bird, very high up, a mere speck. Then, one May morning, when she had risen very early and the smell of summer filled the air, Barley, leaning over her bedroom window saw, nearer than ever it had been, the bird who had kept her company throughout the winter. It was, without a doubt, a skylark.

Acting on a strange and touching impulse, she called, 'Polly, Polly, is it you?'

The bird was singing as though its heart would break. And for several seconds it would not stop. Barley called again.

'Polly, I believe that it is you.'

It was Polly. And suddenly the wearied endless stream of song ceased, and the small bird fell like a stone to the grass in the recreation ground. Barley rushed out and searched in the dewy grass. For many minutes she went round and round the place where she thought the bird had fallen. Then, just as she was about to take one step forward, she heard a tiny voice from the ground.

'Oh Barley, I have finished singing forever. Pick me up, dear. Take me home.'

Barley, wondering whether she were dreaming, picked up the small warm bird, covered it in her hands, and took it home. She laid it on a cushion on the sofa where the bright morning sun shone upon it. The little body was trembling with faint life. Barley knew it must die.

'Oh, Polly dear, can you speak to Barley once again?'

Very, very faint came the answering words, words that were like the tinkle of light rain upon summer leaves.

'Barley, I had to go this way, dear. It had been coming on me for weeks. I tried to stop singing forever. I did not want to leave you. But this was my fate and I knew it. My father told me at one of the séances that my mother had beaten him. There was no music where he had gone to, he said. And he warned me that if I let myself go the same way, I should meet with the same fate. Now, it is the lark who sings at Heaven's gate, dear; and I have done that. During the rehearsals I could not dare to sing. I was too frightened. Not until I got to the beautiful Albert Hall and watched Sir Kenneth could I find my voice again. The moment we stood up I knew something curious was happening to me. I saw Sir Kenneth's baton raised. And then – well, Barley dear, I sang ... and the moment I touched my first note I knew that Polly Ponsonby had ceased to exist as you knew her. I could, of course, have stayed there, perched on Brenda's shoulder perhaps. I did brush my wings against her cheek. But when a lark sings he must rise. And rise I did and found, by merciful providence, a broken pane of glass through which I flew to the Albert Memorial.

'I wanted to let you know, but I could not do so earlier, in case you should tell Rye and he would put me in a cage. It was that which kept me away from you, Barley. Yet all through the winter, when I should, of course, have emigrated, I could not resist singing over my old places. There is nowhere more beautiful than Sydenham in the world, I am sure. I am glad that I stayed. But it has given me a chill from which I shall *not* recover. I don't mind. I have sung my life out as a lark should. And now I go to – nothing, as larks do. It is much better to be a lark than go on wandering round circles as the spiritualists do, or live forever in Heaven as the Christians do – or, as I fear some do, pass to the other place. A lark has the best of both worlds, and by his art of singing gives the very breath of life to his body. Mr Shelley knew all about it. Goodbye, Barley dear. Don't stuff me. Bury me with father's flute.'

With a little shudder the small bird died. And so Polly Ponsonby passed forever away from Baker's Lane.

If you go to the cottage now, a very old lady who lives alone, a Miss Merton, may perhaps be induced to talk of these events. But she prefers to remain silent with her memories.

III

The Sack

It's no use pretending I can go on much longer. I can't. And that is an understatement. Yet I must understate it, try to rationalise it. Get it out of my system. And the only way I can do that is to put it down on paper. For who to read? God knows.

Living alone, I'm well aware that one gets silly ideas. You come back to the house when you've been for a prowl round the park, and it's late afternoon with the sun setting and winter round the corner, as you might say (for it's autumn as I try to write this), and you see a kitchen chair or a saucepan or a shovel left exactly where you left them. And you think – they've been moved. Then, looking back, you realize everything is just as when you went out. Except that it's a bit darker.

And that is what is so awful.

No. That is overstatement. It isn't 'awful'. It's plain ordinary. And yet, the very ordinariness of everything can be frightening. And of course, I've had such a horribly ordinary life. And now, being 'redundant' – that's about as ordinary as you can get in days when inflation drains you and catches you in the stomach, and Mr Rising Price, to use an old-fashioned term, gets you by the short and curlies.

Why did I write 'short and curlies'? Nobody uses that phrase any more. As I see it written down, I realize how out of everything I am – a redundant old fool in his sixties who spent years trapped on the wrong side of the Post Office counter. Not even one hold-up to give an edge to any day.

Years. Yes, years. All those years gone now, and Dorothy gone, and both girls in Canada with their families, and letters on my birthday and at Christmas. They think I'm all right. I suppose I am, really. Just lonely. Is it even worth telling them that I got the sack – which is what being 'redundant' means?

The sack ... The word has crept in. No. It's leapt in, in a way I didn't expect. I'd never even thought of other meanings of the word until I wrote that.

But that is exactly what the thing does. Creeps, and leaps. For all I know, it might strangle.

I don't smoke. I don't drink. And sex is something of the past – not that I ever had much. Oh, I think of sex often. Who doesn't, particularly in these days? Who can escape from it? *Playboy* and so on. And now, *Knave.* I'm sick of it all. I try to read serious books, like Lucretius. Yes, I've tried him, God knows why, except that I remember reading him when I was a lad of sixteen, and other classical writers. Juvenal, for example. Yes, I try to keep my mind on serious matters.

But that Sixth Satire of Juvenal – God! it's strong stuff! And how he hated women ...

It's no use. I'm getting nowhere. I said to myself – I'll sit down and try to relate quite simply what has been happening in the last few days. So I'll start again – perhaps send a copy of this to Pam or Cynthia in Canada.

Are you listening, either of you? Four thousand miles away. Can you hear your old father? If you want the truth, he's crying out loud for help, and doesn't know how to make you hear. I suppose there's nothing really wrong with him. But he doesn't want to be slotted into a home for MDs – he doesn't want to have this electrical treatment they give people like me nowadays, like putting them in a mental cage, it seems to me.

Here are the bare facts.

It began with my neighbour in this respectable avenue in this vile town of Hadderminster where all they do is make carpets and pull down old houses and cottages, and dig up the roads, exposing drains and gas pipes, and generally make a foul mess of what was once not so bad a little place in the Midlands. Here I've lived all my life.

Why did this man have to become my neighbour? He's called Knowles – Kenneth Knowles, but we're not on Christian name terms. It's Mr Knowles and Mr Patch, and always will be. Better that way, really. I can't see him calling me Ted, or me calling him Kenneth, or Ken. No. In the Avenue it's Mister, Mrs, or Miss. Still, there's a feeling of neighbourliness. If I was trapped in the bungalow at night with a fire raging in the hall, Mr Knowles would be on the scene before you could say knife. And I suppose I'd come to his rescue too, if needed.

But why did he have to become my neighbour? I never liked him from the start, when he came here a year ago. Nobody knew anything about him; and his grim-looking sister spoke to nobody, only made me mad with her hideous little yapping dog she keeps locked up all day and only lets out at fixed times to do his jobs. And I know the times; I'm keyed up for them. I can hear that yap in advance, time it exactly.

But all this has nothing to do with what I'm trying to write about. And K. Knowles, for all I know, is a perfectly decent kind of chap. About my age, or a little younger. I don't suppose he really meant me any harm. Other neighbours, people I've known well for years, wondered who he was and what kind of life he'd lived before he bought the house next door. Only I found out.

As I write, it's late at night. I had to stop. I'm hot. The electric heater's on, two bars, in this little breakfast-room where Dorothy and I had all our meals. I've just unbuttoned the collar of my shirt and ripped my tie off. There's a fire laid in the grate, I laid it this morning, then I thought – I don't really need a fire, not in early October. Then it came to evening, and I thought – no, I'll use the electric, it'll save me going to the outhouse, where the sack –

Why didn't anybody teach me, when I was young, to write properly? To put down in clear sentences of good English just what you want to put down? I just can't seem to assemble my thoughts coherently enough to get my story – is it a story? – in order.

So – what? The sack. Yes. I'm writing about a sack – about *The* Sack. The one my neighbour gave me. Now I've got that down, I may be able to stick to facts.

Yesterday, Mr Knowles said to me – no. I don't want to put that down now. I must try to get things in proper order. And it starts with dead leaves.

Dead leaves – the leaves of last autumn, which I'd crammed into a plastic sack and was dragging down to the bottom of the garden, intending to burn them. Dorothy said – keep them for compost. But I just couldn't be bothered with that sort of thing, after she'd gone. So I decided to burn them. And when I think of burning them, I think of ash, and that puts me in mind of ashes and sack-cloth. Funny, how things come together.

He said to me, over the box hedge: 'Mr Patch,' he said, 'Mr Patch, that plastic sack – it's got a hole in it. Try this one.'

And he slung a proper sack over the hedge. It fell at my feet. Proper sack? What do I mean by that? I mean, an old-fashioned sack – made of 'coarse material', to use a dictionary definition. The kind of sack I've known so well for so many years. The sack the postman uses.

It seemed to me presumptuous of him, if that's the right word. For I didn't really need his sack. But the way he'd slung it at me – there was a kind of contempt in the gesture. He's a tall, very well-built man; and it was only me who found out (one gets to ways of finding out things when one's worked in the Post Office for years) that he'd been in the CID. Once I'd got that established, a lot about him that had seemed mysterious, fell together. Those wide shoulders, huge hands, sturdy legs, and cunning eyes ... Yes. He'd lived a dangerous life, no doubt about it. And now, retired, with that grim sister, it could be boring for him. In a way, I admire him. I felt – this is the kind of anonymous man who protects people like me. And never gets much of a reward – except, I suppose, a feeling of satisfaction when he's run somebody to earth. There's a pride about him I understand. For even I have my pride – after years of doing out 'special issues' and going slower when you see there's a queue building up the other side of the counter. You develop pride, that way. And you learn to be patient.

As for K. Knowles – I suppose he needed patience too, a different kind of patience, a predatory kind of patience, eager for the pounce, then swooping down, like a hawk. Oh yes, I do admire him, even if I hate him for dropping that sack in my path, and knowing quite well what he was doing.

I *know* he knew what he was doing.

But what did the sack do? that is what I'm trying to put down. And – what is it doing now?

All my life I've felt that what they call 'inanimate' objects have a life of their own. 'Of their own?' Do I mean that? Not exactly. I mean – a life in relation to what are called 'animate' objects. A much slower life; but stealthy. As a child, I remember watching a chunk of coal burn, and then suddenly sizzle or sparkle in the grate, and then fuse into flame, only to die, and become a clinker by morning. I used to say to myself – that was an 'inanimate' object only an hour ago, before it went into the grate and the match was struck. So, all my life I've questioned 'inanimate' objects. A leaf, for example. A dead leaf. Or a candle, before flame touches the wick, and the wax curls. A chair. A spoon. Inanimates? And – a sack?

I *am* right. Take stone, even the most ancient stone. Those at Stonehenge, say. Does one call them 'inanimate?' Of course, it could be proved that the stones on Salisbury Plain have been there for thousands of years. But are they exactly the same now as the stones which were dragged there, inch by inch, from Pembrokeshire? Only a dolt who believed that the stars didn't revolve, could believe that. Lucretius says a lot about this kind of thing, somewhere.

Anyway, this sack. I just said, 'Oh, thank you, Mr Knowles.' And picking it up, as he went back to his house, I threw it in the garage – empty now, except for garden tools, logs and a lawnmower and odds and ends; for I had to give up the car.

It was then, when I first picked it up, that I began to itch.

It's odd, and I suppose irrelevant. But I ask myself, what would the sack have done if I'd still got the car and used it on a cold night to cover the engine with? Perhaps that is what they call a 'rhetorical' question. No answer needed. And yet – what would it have done to the engine of the old Riley?

I can't go on writing. I have to go to the outhouse, and see what the sack is doing. But no. In writing that down, I begin to see how crazy I've become. I'm a 'case'. Because, of course, the thing will be there, where I left it. Or, did I leave it there, in the outhouse, by the coal and sticks? Did I? I cannot remember.

I think it's wiser not to move from here. Yes. I won't go away from this table until I've written down what I know is true. I will *not* go to the outhouse.

I'm getting my thoughts in order. This is what I have to put down. First: a day after I'd thrown the sack in the garage (and locked the doors as I always do, even though I've no car), I opened the back door, next morning, to take in the usual pinta, and – there was the sack.

Put down plain like that, it reads so simple it seems to mean nothing; and maybe it does mean nothing. Maybe I didn't leave the sack in the garage. Maybe I left it outside, and the wind lifted it to the back door, to huddle up over the one milk bottle. Like a lurker.

It's odd, now I come to think of it, how I used that word 'huddle' – for that is exactly what it did. It had arranged itself over the milk bottle, as though it needed sustenance. Yes, sustenance. The sack was starved. It needed milk. It came to the milk.

That is how it seemed to me, ten days ago. But still, I said to myself (before the later events came to pass) I must have imagined that I locked it up in the garage.

And so, I took the milk bottle in, picked up the sack, and as I did so there was a little whip and snarl of wind, suddenly veered to the north – biting cold. A wind with teeth in it. I dropped the sack, came in quickly, and locked the door. Early morning; but one likes to be on the safe side. The milkman had told me that there was a lurker around. And living alone, you get used to locking up, even in the morning.

Later that same day, I went out. Sack not there. At first, that signified nothing. For why should it be there, with a howling wind striding from the north?

I thought no more of it, but walked to the bakery, to get bread. It was only on the way back, happening to look up to the one chimney on the bungalow, that I began to ask myself – *had* I left the sack in the garage the night before?

Because now, it was curled round the chimney and the TV aerial. Draping itself over the tiles, in a kind of graceful manner, almost protective, as though it had settled there for the winter.

Yet I still told myself – the wind did it. Until the wind dropped and in a dead quietness when even the withering roses – the white roses Dorothy loved so much – till even the white rose petals didn't quiver, I saw the sack hunched up, or should I say 'bunched' up, against the front door, the door I now never use, not even for the Vicar should he happen to call, as he once did, not long after Dorothy went. There it was; and when I write 'hunched' or 'bunched' – I mean – in a kind of pyramid, or a tent, as though three sticks had been stood up inside, wigwam-fashion, holding it tent-wise. Like a little tabernacle.

I wish I hadn't used that word, 'tabernacle'. For even as I wrote it I half knew what it meant. And now I've looked it up in *Chambers*. 'A tent, or movable hut ... or, the human body as the temporary abode of the soul ...'

It was not until then – not until I saw the sack slooped against my front door, as though it was saying, 'Let me in, please ...' – it was not until then that I was certain: I *had* left it, in the locked garage, the night before.

From that moment, I knew I was not just imagining things. From that moment, my life has become a torment.

But I must not overstate. In a kind of way, I've learnt to live with it, learnt to live with this torment, this bit of 'coarse material', dun grey with a slither of rustiness in it, and a prickly roughness that seems to tinge the fingers. Learnt to live with it – yes. But I cannot easily touch it. For one thing, I'm now convinced that this itching I get, all over my body, was caused by contact with the sack. There's a kind of tic in it. Yes, a tic.

But I am not really writing of physical matters, although one cannot discountenance them. So – what happened next?

I think it was this way. After I'd seen the sack before the

front door, I decided it might be a good thing to open the door and let the sun into the hall. And when I did – well, I opened the door to nothing. Or, rather, only to the rose bushes in the bed near the door. The sack had been blown away.

Why did I write 'blown away'? I suppose I am still trying to rationalize. In fact, there was, as I've said, no wind at all. The sack could not have been blown away. And, certainly, it could not have been 'blown' into the house, where I found it, late that night, lying in a slither, along the bottom of the door to a cupboard where I keep all the odds and ends everybody keeps. The things you want to lose, and can't lose.

I didn't sleep well that night. This is unusual for me – and I never take sleeping pills. But I tossed about a lot; and when I write that – I mean it in the old sense. I mean, I was sexually alert. And I awoke about three – bad hour, I've heard people say. And so it is. I awoke to feel myself stiffening, and hot; and the bed-clothes all in a tumble about me. There had been a bad dream; but, what was it? I couldn't remember. And there was a foul yet sweet smell, which I couldn't place. Was it sweat? Was it my own smell? I didn't know. Somehow, with bones that ached and creaked, I jerked my body up from the bed.

I stood for a moment, trembling all over. I was looking at what lay, crinkled and frozen, over the candlewick spread.

It was then I fully realized – the sack was an enemy. It was *the* enemy.

I am determined to go on writing, not to go to the out-house. I am determined to put down what I know is true.

But I wish I wasn't alone here.

What happened next that night? I stood by the bed, and I must have picked up the sack, I must have – or *did* I? Did I pick it up? This is what I can't remember. What I do remember is that I went to the toilet, and was sick, violently sick, and then went to the medicine cupboard and found a bottle of sleeping tablets, which the doctor had prescribed for my wife, in her last months. I had always meant to throw them into the dust-bin; but now I took one, and never having taken sleeping pills before, I was soon in a dead sleep.

I think I dreamt of Dorothy. I don't know. But it seemed another age when I woke up, although it was really only another day. I didn't let myself think of the sack – not until about four in the afternoon, when I went into the front room, a room I hardly ever use now.

Why did I go there, anyway? What sent me? I think it was a message from my wife. I think she said to me, 'Ted, go and dust my picture.' Her picture – a fine pencil drawing of her head, as a young girl, one of our treasures, hangs above the fireplace in the front room. And when I went in there ...

It seems unnecessary to write it down.

Again, I cannot remember removing the sack. I don't think I touched it. I do remember smut on the glass of the picture. Then I closed the door, and came to where I am now, and sat down, and tried to think of it all calmly.

It is so difficult to write calmly of the movements of the sack in these last days. I can't get them in proper order. In the bath, one night; but which night? Never again on the bed. And that was kind of it. Then for two whole days I saw no sign of it. And I said to myself, pathetic really, the wind has snaffled it away.

I wish I had been right. I wish I hadn't come in the next day, after I had been down to the PO to draw my pension – I wish I hadn't come in to see it laid flat upon the table where now I write all this.

Flat, yes, flat. Except for two little mounds, that reminded me of breasts. But otherwise, quite flat, as though it had been pressed, almost ironed out.

For the first time, without touching it, I looked very closely at the coarse woven material. I cannot have imagined it. I could see the shapes of bones in the material. 'Rag and bones' – the call came from my childhood. I remember no more – except that I ran out of the room, out of the house, only longing to feel the autumn air upon me.

And was that the last I saw of it? No, it cannot have been. Since I know now that it is, or should be, in the outhouse. And when I write 'should be' I mean only that it was there this morning, over the coal. It looked as though it had crawled there.

I must not go out to check on this. I must first tell how I went to my neighbour, and talked about it.

'Mr Knowles,' I said, 'Mr Knowles – ' And then I stopped. I could see that something in my expression, or my tone of voice, had got him. 'Come in,' was all he said. And in his sitting-room, where his sister sat silent and aware, doing a jig-saw puzzle on a little antique table, he said to me, 'What's the trouble?'

I knew he knew what the 'trouble' was. And so it was easy simply to say, 'The sack'.

There was not the smallest change of expression in his face.

'Yes,' he said. 'I realize.' And then a long pause, and the sister went on doggedly searching out another piece for her jig-saw.

'You *realize*?' I said. He merely nodded.

There was a long silence, till at last he asked me to sit down. I didn't. I felt aggrieved. I felt, for sure, that he had done me wrong; and that he knew it.

I started to speak. I wanted to protest. I wanted to say, 'That sack you gave me – '

But he got in first. 'I'm sorry.' That is how he began. And I could see he was sorry.

Suddenly, his sister got up. 'Would you like a cup of coffee?' She left the room before I could answer; and I never saw the coffee. Because the brother so quickly spoke, and I so quickly left the house, when I heard what he had to tell me.

'I shouldn't have given it to you,' he said. And then, in a blank kind of voice, as though it really meant nothing to him: 'It has a history. I shouldn't have kept it. I always knew that. It should have been destroyed. If you remember, the Cassenden case – six years ago. I was in charge of that. A sex-killer – and we have our own names for them just as, I daresay, Mr Patch, you had your own names in the Post Office business?'

I could only nod. And let him go on.

'We got him, perhaps you remember, on one murder only. Please believe me, I never talk about such matters. But now

I have to. The girl – she was only nineteen – was dismembered. The dismembered body was found in Wyre Forest. The sack – 'And I remember that here he hesitated, and at that moment I could hear his sister, the other side of the door. But she did not come in, and I guessed she was listening. 'The sack contained the remains.'

'Why did you throw it to me?' I almost shouted at him. And Mr Knowles looked at me gravely.

'I don't know.' That was all he said. Then a pause, and that sister still shuffling, the other side of the door. And Mr Knowles went on: 'I had to get rid of it somehow. It – 'And here there was a long silence.' – Gave me a bit of trouble.'

'But surely – ' I protested, 'surely – such gruesome relics – you didn't usually keep such things?'

'No,' he agreed. 'No. We don't. But in this case – and I was a long time on it, if you remember – in this case, I asked finally if I could keep the sack. It was a symbol of a sort of victory for me.' Then again, a silence, until he added, 'I always regret I did keep it.'

'So the sack contained – ?' I began a question I could not finish. But Mr Knowles finished it for me.

'It contained – the legs, the arms, the abdomen, part of the neck. But it did not contain – '

I ran out of his house, before the sister could bring the coffee. But as I slammed his door I heard her speaking angrily to him.

'You fool. Why did you have to tell him?'

I didn't wait to hear more. This was yesterday. And now ... now ...

I wish I weren't alone in this place. I sit here snug and warm with the electric heater on in this little breakfast-room. Both doors, to the hall and to the scullery, are closed. It is October, and I hear the rustle of dead leaves outside on a cold, clear night, without wind. The white rose is dead. I've neglected it, I've neglected everything.

I think I'd better light the fire, save electricity. But if I do it'll mean going to the outhouse to get more coal. Still, if I lit it, and let it die, and saw only ash, white ash like the white rose, I might feel better. I feel, so strangely, my innocence upon me – and what do I mean by that? I mean that I would like to go back to my earliest days, before I knew right from wrong.

I must get up from this table. I can't write any more. I think I must light the fire. For I can't go to bed. It is so lonely in bed.

I remember something else Mr Knowles said to me. 'Burn it,' he said. 'Burn it.' And then he added, quietly, 'If you can.'

... I've lit the fire, and been out to get more coal. I have come back. I didn't bring any coal. The sack was still there, where it was this morning. Rolled up into a kind of ball. I touched it with my foot.

It was hard.

IV

Art Thou Languid?

They had been in business together for over twenty years, a partnership that was broken, first, by the departure of Mr Hoare to his native town in Yorkshire (in 1941), and, very soon after, by the death of Mr Weary. So, for the last time, the shutters were put up to the music shop on Calverley Hill and the names were almost forgotten, commemorated only by those who knew a little of the inner history of the partners, and by the words themselves – Weary and Hoare – painted in blue and gold letters above the long peeling shutters of the bay windows. Inside the shop the stacks of music, the gramophone records, the busts of famous composers, the Bechstein piano behind the door (by whose means Mr Hoare had liked to interpret the 'Valse Triste' of Sibelius) – all these, and even the account books, it is said, remain untouched, in exactly the same position – though in more decaying a condition – as on the day, four years earlier, when Mr Weary was forced to retire, a dying man, to his bed.

The shop is curiously isolated in a road that leads steeply out of the cathedral town of Wellsborough and has become the resort of the prosperous, who, within our times, built large houses, ornate and complacent, with extensive ornamental gardens. Isolated as much by age as by position: for it knew the days of Queen Anne and was once the post-office of Calverley village. But isolated also for other reasons which the prosperous householders of Calverley Hill do not much care to talk about. Nobody will be found – except perhaps in the cathedral close, where such things are trifled with – to declare it to be haunted. Neither will anyone, returning home at tea-time on a tempestuous afternoon of late autumn, linger to light a

cigarette in the padlocked doorway of the shop, or take protection there from a sudden downwash of hail. For the 'Valse
Triste' is still heard from the piano on the other side of that
door where dead leaves, mingled with the tattered leaves of
music which have slipped through from the darkened shop,
rustle and crackle in the wind.

The names, ludicrous and full of lassitude, were the natural
bonds which united them: the names, a melancholy winter
afternoon, a funeral, and a canal barge. In January of 1918,
when most people's energies were at a low ebb, Harold Weary
and Lionel Hoare, both natives of Haggerley Ford, a small
town in the West Riding, were on fourteen days' leave from
the mud of France. Lionel, then a man of thirty, unmarried,
going a little stout, with clear blue eyes and a quick confid-
ing smile, was organist at the parish church. In the trenches,
while his comrades showed one another photographs of their
girls, Lionel dreamt of his three-manual organ and burnt with
desire to feel his fingers curl over the Great Double Trumpet.
He was fond of women, but too shy and modest to advance
any further with them than a longing smile. During his leave,
which he spent with his parents, the vicar of the church died
and Lionel played at the funeral. The choir-boys attended,
and a handful of men, amongst them Harold Weary, a thin and
wistful-looking man, five years younger than Hoare.

Weary was one of those emotionally uneasy men, sardonic
from self-consciousness, who are naturally the bait of schoolboys. The Vicar's favourite hymn, 'Art thou weary, art thou
languid?', sung at the funeral, invited an obvious joke from one
of the boys, who, turning round in his stall, indecently bawled
the line directly at Harold. Afterwards, in the vestry, another
boy came up to him and, with an assumption of innocence,
said: 'Please, sir?'

'Well, what?' snapped Harold.

In a kindly voice, distant as a lark, the lad continued: 'Art
thou languid, sir?'

This was the prearranged signal for all the others to cry,

'No, he's weary!', which they did with great zest, as they tumbled out into the churchyard and the damp mist of an afternoon already threatened by night.

Lionel Hoare, carefully hanging up his ARCO hood on the peg in his cupboard, laughed and turned to Harold. But Harold was scowling and had obviously not cared for the joke.

'You mustn't take it so seriously,' said Lionel.

'But it's *true*,' said Harold. 'I *am* weary. I *am* languid.'

He spoke with a passion which impressed the other man and even frightened him a little.

'What's in a name?' said Lionel. 'Look at mine! They rag me no end in the Army.'

'Don't talk to me about the Army.'

But it was in comparing their service experiences that the two men, walking home together along the banks of the canal, came to find something akin to an affection for one another. It wasn't really affection, nor any common qualities of character, which brought them together. It was the similarity of their circumstances; for both of them were tired and both of them longed to escape.

Then they saw the barge, a looming shadow floating along the colourless water of the canal, and painted on the stern the word 'Atlantis'.

'Atlantis,' said Harold. 'That's supposed to be the name of a lost island.'

'Wish we could find it,' muttered Lionel. He stared straight before him at the towering shoulder of hills which pressed formidably over the canal.

'Maybe we could, you and me,' said Harold.

Lionel laughed, that warm chuckle in his throat which came as the sudden hint of a buried personality. 'Weary and Hoare! That's good!' He spluttered with laughter. It seemed to him the craziest thing he had ever imagined – Weary and Hoare landing on Atlantis. But when he stopped laughing he saw Harold's heavy, brooding eyes turned on him and again he had a sense of fear, an unreasonable fear which curiously thrilled and satisfied him. In that second, silently, a relationship was born and accepted: Harold, the vessel of the imagination, Lionel, the pilot – yet always subservient to the stronger will of the younger man.

'Atlantis is where you make it,' said Harold.

'What do you mean, old man?'

But Harold preferred not to explain. To do so would be to admit that secretly, for years, he had written poetry; verses that no magazine editor would glance at, but to the writer his very life's blood. 'Can you bear the thought of coming back here to live when the war's over?' he asked.

'Oh – I don't know – not so bad – '

But then Harold gripped his arm. The pressure seemed to squeeze out of Lionel that half-acknowledged dread which lay always at the back of his mind – the dread of returning home, the only son of over-loving parents, to resume a life that war had shattered in a way they could never understand. 'Tell you the truth,' he muttered unwillingly, 'I don't want the war to end.'

'Yes, you do. But you don't want to come back here.'

Smoke from collieries drifted over the canal. In it both men saw the firm outlines of their slain boyhood. But when the smoke cleared they saw only the drab roofs of the small town, incredibly dreary and hopeless.

'I've saved a little money,' began Lionel. 'I thought ...' He hesitated, then he burst out, 'If I left here, 'twould break up the folks at home.'

'Damn the folks at home! Haven't they broken up us?'

'You're not married, I suppose?'

Harold laughed. 'Marry – and bring kids into a world like this! No, Mr Hoare, I'm not married, nor ever will be.'

'You got parents?'

'They're dead. I live with an old aunt.'

'What job had you got, lad, before the war?'

'Behind the counter at Henderson's, the tailor.'

'He'd have you back, I suppose?'

'I wouldn't go.'

'I was a clerk in Spalding's, the steel people. They told all our chaps they were keeping jobs open for them.'

'A man who can play the organ like you — what do you want to be a clerk for, Mr Hoare?'

'You can't live on music.'

'You could. You could sell music. That's something we both know about, something we could do.'

Lionel chuckled. 'Weary and Hoare — it sounds so damn' silly.'

'Depends how you look at it. To me it sounds right, like bacon and eggs, or chalk and cheese.'

He looked at Lionel and wondered what it was that had attracted him to the older man and drawn the suggestion from him. Was it a certain cherubic innocence about him, which flattered his own sleeping paternal instinct?

Then Lionel looked over his shoulder along the misty canal where the darkening winter day had already turned to night. He shivered. 'Let's get home. It's dreary here.'

'You look as though you've seen a ghost,' said Harold.

'Funny you should say that. When I was a kid about eight I heard somebody scream here one night. I'll never forget it. Never found out who it was. But I always used to believe it was a ghost.'

'And you're still frightened of ghosts? Is that it?' Harold spoke urgently. He felt as though he must protect Lionel.

'Oh no, of course not. Don't believe in such things now. Come along. I want my tea.' Lionel went ahead along the towing-path, Harold following him, picking his steps carefully through the black mud. Occasionally Lionel turned his head to make sure that the other man was following. He was always there, a few inches behind.

In the evening Harold, reading Swinburne while his aunt knitted a comforter, saw in the vibrant words of the poet the bland, warm and slightly mischievous face of Lionel Hoare. A sense of power exalted him. For the first time in his life he felt that he had found another human being whom he could com-

mand. Sitting there, his eyes upon the book, he willed Lionel
to throw in his lot with him. He did not want the music shop.
He wanted, as a cat wants, something to play with, some toy
which could occupy the long bleak days ahead. He began to
love the older man, as an artist loves the work he is making.

Lionel, at that moment trying a new piece on the piano in
his parents' sitting-room, stopped suddenly and went to the
hall for his hat and coat. 'Going out a bit,' he said to his parents.

'Ay, lad. Enjoy yersel'.' His father smiled.

'What was that music, lad?' asked his mother.

'Valse Triste,' said Lionel, 'by Sibelius.'

'And *triste* it is,' said his father.

'Your Dad likes to air his French,' said his mother. They
began to chaff one another good-humouredly. Lionel, leaving
the house and climbing the narrow cobbled hill towards Harold's aunt's house, longed for a wife who would chaff him. He
had always liked being teased.

The two men spent that evening, and almost every other
evening of their leave, in the saloon bar of the Goat and Thistle.
It was with a drugged sense of inevitability that they discussed
ways and means for their project, Lionel – the business mind of
the two – working out figures on slips of paper and comparing
the advantages of one town over another.

On the last night of their leave, Lionel said, 'Are we really
going to do this, Harold?'

'We are.'

'Why? Doesn't it strike you as queer?'

Harold looked at Lionel's honest, bewildered face. 'If you
back out on this,' he muttered, 'I'll kill myself. And then I'll
haunt you.'

Again the intensity, the note of hysteria, frightened and fascinated Lionel. 'Don't be an idiot,' he said. 'Why should I back
out? Provided we find the right premises, I'm with you.'

'To Weary and Hoare,' said Harold, raising his glass.

'Two damn' tired old soldiers,' echoed Lionel.

Both of them knew that in trying to escape from the circumstances of their world they had fettered their lives to one

another. They were neither happy nor unhappy; yet happier than they had been before their meeting, happier in a dulled condition of irresponsibility. For they had resigned themselves to the mythical will of fate, that tyrant which lies in the hearts of all men and, once obeyed, becomes the master.

In the midsummer of that tired year Lionel was wounded in the thigh. The wound was not serious, though for the rest of his life he was to endure the discomfort of a right leg that would succumb, an easy victim, to the insidious dampness of the south-west wind.

He was sent to a country mansion, near Wellsborough, which had been adapted as a hospital. After some weeks, when he was again able to walk, he came daily to enjoy the many mediaeval charms of the cathedral city.

Later, he knew that these were the happiest weeks of his life. Wellsborough was exactly the kind of town, so mild and mellow, so much of a contrast to Haggerley Ford, which could give him the benison he needed. Under its influence he ripened like an apple that had been in danger of withering. He got to know the cathedral organist and often sat with him in the loft, though he never ventured to play, for he was too out of practice; his weak leg made it impossible for him to use the pedals, and he was too modest to speak to his host – a benign Cambridge doctor – of his own considerable skill. He would, after Evensong, take tea in a fifteenth-century café which had once been part of a monastic house. From his window seat, misted by the idle August sun, he would watch the grave central towers of the cathedral and the rooks, those reincarnated religious of cathedral towns, about their noisy business in the high elms. Always for tea he had a boiled egg, brown bread-and-butter, and a slice of plain, home-made cake. And he fell in love – not for the first time, but this time more courageously and with more hope of success, for his healthy smiling face and his honoured hospital blue made an appeal to the pretty waitress, called Ilona, who daily served him.

One afternoon, the early-closing day, he took her for a

walk and they sat by the banks of the river, watching other lovers in punts and dinghies. He put his arm round her waist. 'You don't mind!' he asked. No, she didn't mind, of course she didn't, she thought he was sweet. He walked back under the lime-trees, silently holding her hand, so blissfully happy that he could not speak. 'See you tomorrow,' he said, as he mounted his bus. She nodded and waved to him.

But next day Ilona's mother was ill and she was not at the café. He thought of asking for her address and calling on her; but it seemed, he thought, a forward thing to do. Instead, after tea, he wandered some way up Calverley Hill, intending to pick up his bus at the top. And so he found the shuttered shop, high on the slopes of a valley, with its long narrow orchard tapering down behind it and its door plastered by a notice which announced the sale of this highly desirable period premises.

He knew at once – and at once he saw the music displayed in the windows, he heard the sound of a piano from inside, he saw – with heart-breaking clarity – Ilona pegging up clothes in the orchard. But then he saw, in place of the words 'Williams and Son, Drapers' above the windows, the fateful names 'Weary and Hoare'. And Ilona, cheerfully carrying her basket of clothes to the orchard, faded out.

The two were incompatible, that was obvious. But the shop, and this view of the luscious valley with its mother cathedral in the meadows – this was his. He inquired next from the agent. More money was needed than he had saved. He was not the sort of man to consider a loan, it did not even enter his mind. Neither did he ever seriously consider that in wiring to Harold Weary and keeping faith with their bargain he was cutting Ilona forever out of his life. Somewhere, he vaguely believed, a place must be found for her.

For the next two days, waiting a reply from Harold, he did not go to the café. Was it perhaps possible, he asked himself, that Harold no longer wanted to go on with their plan? He had heard nothing from him since the early spring when a post-card reached him in France, which had read: 'Don't forget our contract. I'm keeping my eyes open for a place.' This was from a hospital in the Midlands. Lionel had replied, but no further letter had come. For all Lionel knew, Harold might be dead. 'But I'd know,' muttered Lionel, 'I'm sure I'd know if he were dead.' And he wondered vaguely why he was so certain of that.

Then a telegram came. *Invalided out. Book room. Coming tomorrow.*

Lionel met him and was shocked at his haggard face and shrunken stoop. But Harold did not want to talk of his illness. He immediately agreed that the shop would do. That was all he said.

'It'll do.'

'But don't you think it's wonderful?'

'Ay. It's all right.'

'And the cathedral quite near, and – oh, I wish you'd be more enthusiastic!'

'I'm not a fellow who shows his enthusiasm.' But Harold's eyes lit and he seized Lionel's arm. 'I knew you'd never go back on me,' he said.

They went to the agent and paid their deposit. Afterwards, searching for a place to have tea, Harold pointed to the café with its leaning timbered front.

'This looks your sort of place. Old-fashioned and that.'

'No, not there,' said Lionel. 'The food's not up to much.'

He felt as though he had plunged a sword through his own heart as they sat in the palm-lounge of the Clevedon Hotel discussing the business before them.

A week later Lionel returned home, and Harold with him. He never saw Ilona again. She had left Wellsborough by the time, in the spring of 1919, they came to occupy the shop.

The business started favourably. Almost their first customer was Dr Rothway, the cathedral organist, who had grown to like Lionel. There had been, of course, another music shop in the town; but the war had closed its doors and Weary and Hoare were soon accepted in its place. Puffing up Calverley Hill for his daily afternoon walk, the doctor often dropped in, perhaps to order Harwood's latest organ piece, or merely to have a chat and air his favourite grievance – the non-musical Dean. This was sufficient to give prestige to the new business. Lionel, quick to realize the possibilities, earnestly studied the publishers' catalogues and ordered copies of every new piece of church music by any composer of distinction. The precentor, a young man, an enemy of the aged doctor, got the Weary and Hoare habit. It was his pleasure to drop in and try new piano music on one of the upright Rogers pianos.

It was the exciting period of gramophone development and before the days of radio. By 1925 one side of the shop had been turned into a small studio, with a sound-proof wall, where records could be played. Elena Gerhardt, Elizabeth Schumann, Gervase Elwes, Galli-Curci – these, and other heavenly voices, soared out into the shop from Columbia and His Master's Voice. Portraits of modern composers filled the walls; busts of the great classical giants surmounted the high shelves. Miniature orchestral scores were added to stock. The lighter side of music was ignored. No jazz or ragtime ever found its way to Weary and Hoare. Albums of hackneyed classics – Tchaikovski, Rubinstein, Weber – were the only concessions made to lower brows. Boys from the Cathedral School, some of the lay-clerks, the cathedral clergy themselves – all came to regard a visit to Weary and Hoare as something more than a mere visit to a shop. Cathedral tittle-tattle floated across the counter, for Lionel was one of those men who invite confidences, obviously discreet, and, in any case, unimportant enough to entrust with a scandal.

He was kept far too busy in those early years ever to ask himself whether he were content with his life. Hardly a day was ever spent out of Wellsborough, and many of the evenings he would be occupied with the accounts and business correspondence, while his partner, precise at domestic tasks, saw to the housekeeping. They kept a strict time-table. At nine-thirty the shop opened. From nine to nine-thirty the two men walked, generally down the hill, once round the cathedral close, and back again. At ten a woman came to do the rougher

housework and shopping. During the morning Lionel looked
after the counter. Until eleven Harold retired to an attic room
which he had made his own private sanctum and where he
continued to write his poetry – verses which were never seen
by Lionel. At eleven he came down to the kitchen and started
to prepare lunch. They closed shop from one to two-fifteen,
eating their lunch in the kitchen while Harold read the newspapers and offered acid commentaries on the events of the day.
While Harold looked after the shop, Lionel cleared away the
lunch. By three o'clock, their busiest time, both men were to
be found in the shop. On Sundays Harold spent the day in
bed, reading the papers and the many strange books which,
slowly, he had collected in his room. They were books on such
subjects as serpent-worship, alchemy, astrology – all the abra-
cadabra of an imagination arrested in adolescence. Slowly he
became a mine of curious facts – tags of which he would drop
out at incongruous moments.

'There were people in Malekula who used to eat their
dead,' he remarked once, lolling in the doorway of the bath-
room while Lionel was shaving.

'Were there?' Lionel chuckled. 'Well, thank Heaven we've
progressed beyond that, anyway.'

'I don't know that we have. It's not a bad way of getting rid
of corpses.'

'There's cremation.'

But the word 'cremation' fired Harold to sudden anger.
'When I die, don't you dare to cremate me.'

'Oh, all right. Anyway, I shall konk out before you. I'm five
years older.'

'No. You'll hang on after me. Quite a long time too.'

Lionel carefully cleaned his razor. 'Why're you so opposed
to cremation?' he asked.

'I want my body to go the natural way.'

Lionel went to his bedroom to dress. He did not spend a very
easy day. The remark 'I want my body to go the natural way'
kept coming back to him. What *was* the natural way of a body
after death – particularly when it was Harold's?

And he remembered again (what he had never really forgotten) an earlier remark, made years ago: 'Then I shall haunt you.'

As the years passed Weary and Hoare became each other's habit, and could not have escaped even had it occurred to them to try. Their names, inscribed by themselves in the book of fate, were chains around them. By 1930, when the business was practically running itself and the balance-sheet showing a nice profit, Lionel, then a man of forty-two, knew one morning of summer when he woke to hear the cuckoo in the orchard that he had incarcerated his life in the tomb of security; and that Harold Weary had hammered the nails into the coffin. He did not know precisely why this revelation had suddenly come to him, unless it were the recollection of Delius's nostalgic piece, 'On Hearing the First Cuckoo in Spring,' which floated into his mind from hearing the cuckoo in the orchard and made him rise from the lonely couch of the last twelve years thinking of the wife who might have shared it and the children who should now be growing up to inherit the fruits of his labour. He felt suddenly old; and, as always when he was unhappy, his right leg began to ache.

At breakfast he opened a letter from his father.

'I must go to Haggerley Ford,' he said, when he had read it.

Harold stared at him. 'Go? You can't. How can I manage here alone?'

'My mother's dying, Harold.'

'So am I.'

'You – ' Lionel stared at the white face. He noticed, for the first time, a pastel bloom in the sallow cheeks.

'Yes. I never told you. I'm t.b.' Harold coughed, as though to demonstrate the truth of what he had said. 'That's why they discharged me from the Army. I knew it years ago. I knew it before I met you. There are no old bones in Harold Weary.'

'But – why on earth don't you see a doctor?'

'You want me to die, don't you?'

'Don't be so silly!'

'Is it silly?'

'Of course it is. I certainly *don't* want you to die.'

'No.' Harold looked at him, struck by a new thought. A secretive smile flickered round the thin lips. 'Of *course* you don't. I never realized.'

'Realized what?'

Harold wouldn't answer. Instead, 'Does it ever strike you,' he asked, 'that this house might be haunted?'

'I don't believe in such things as ghosts.'

'Yes, you do. You're terrified of them. Ever since you heard that scream on the canal as a kid.'

'Don't be so damn' silly!' Lionel's leg gave a sudden twinge of pain. Harold, ignoring him, went on: 'It's the attic stairs, isn't it – where I work? That's the place you don't like.'

Then Lionel's temper burst out. 'My mother's dying,' he cried, 'and you start this sort of talk. You're too damned selfish, that's the trouble. I'm leaving today and you've jolly well got to look after the place yourself. Do you good! You'll have less time for those ridiculous poems you keep saying you're working on but which nobody ever sees.'

'I'll thank you to attack me. Not my poems.'

'Oh, this is a silly argument. Pull yourself together, Harold, for God's sake.'

'There's nothing to pull together. I'm a sick man.'

'I don't believe it. If you took more exercise and stopped reading all those unhealthy books, you'd be a different man. You're not ill. You're weary. That's all.' Into Lionel's mind came an image; a choir-boy in the vestry of a Yorkshire church. 'Art thou languid?' he sneered.

He saw Harold slowly rising from the table. Then he ran upstairs to pack his bag, crying, as he ran, a mocking, inane echo of the choirboys' taunt: 'No, he's weary! No, he's weary!'

Resentment filled Harold Weary as he heard again those words which had always hung in his mind. For indeed he felt, he had always felt, tired to death – and knew, and had always known, that he had been born only to die. But was not death also the gateway to his true vocation? Now he knew, with absolute certainty, that he would haunt Lionel Hoare; and he knew, too, that Lionel both expected it and dreaded it. For what could be the ultimate purpose of their partnership, except that Hoare should be haunted by the ghost of Weary? The uneasy look along the canal, the fear in the bright eyes ... Harold smiled, then chuckled, then fell to a fit of harsh coughing. How glorious the future was going to be!

Capriciously, his mind pointed to another mood; he realized with embittered tenderness how much he loved this friend. Even though he had been so cruelly hurt by him, could he, in *cold blood* (the aptness of the phrase pleased him), submit him to such a fate? Yet how could he be spared? For, once dead, Harold knew that he would have no control over his movements. There was no escape for the wretched Lionel. A ghost must walk where his fate lay.

He stood at the table, fingering a bread-knife, tormented by the thought of the inevitable torments he must inflict, and would enjoy inflicting, upon his only true friend. He was not a cruel man; he did not desire such a fate for Lionel. But what escape could there be for him?

There was only one certain escape. Lionel must die before him.

As soon as that thought entered his mind he was filled with compassion for his friend. Quickly he went upstairs, anxious only to appease him.

'Lionel, I'm sorry.' Lionel was wrapping shoes in newspaper and did not look up. 'Forgive me. You must go away – of course you must. Only – come back. Don't desert me. I'm too proud to tell anyone else what I told you. I knew even as a kid that I wouldn't live long. That's why I wanted a friend like you, someone healthy and normal. I don't envy you your good health. When I die you'll have the shop – you'll have *everything*.' He paused and could not resist a smile; so much was implied in the word 'everything'. 'You won't be too old to marry,' he added. He thought a wife would help Lionel to bear the burden of his haunting.

It was as though the laugh of Ilona had tumbled in the

room. Lionel for a moment could not speak. Then he took Harold's hand. 'Chuck it, old man!' he said. 'Talk to me about anything, but not about getting married. There! Of course I'll come back. And we'll get you well somehow.'

He whistled the tune of the 'Valse Triste' as he continued his packing.

The mother died, the father went to live with some friends, and Lionel, after three weeks in old haunts, decided to spend a few days in London before returning to Wellsborough. He wanted, if only for a short while, the gaiety and exuberance of a great town.

He found, easily enough, what he chiefly wanted; found it by mistake, when he was slightly drunk and wandering back to his hotel towards midnight. He was easy and obvious prey and the girl was kind to him, particularly sympathetic to the pain in his leg.

Afterwards, his conscience hammered at him. 'It's a sin,' he kept saying, 'a sin.' But he giggled as he said it.

'Sin be damned,' said the girl. 'You wanted me and I found you. So what? Nobody's come to no harm that I know of.'

Nobody, he thought, except the dim figure of a girl pegging-up clothes in an orchard; nobody, except unborn children. But what did that matter now? It was hypocritical to pretend that he hadn't enjoyed this back-room business.

So he returned to Wellsborough, a man with a different view of life, who had lost a mother, gained for one night a paid lover, and assumed, without knowing it, the swagger that such adventures beget. He felt that now nothing very much mattered; he would, he decided, do what he damn' well pleased.

He was amazed to find the shop gleaming with new paint and distemper, inside and out, and the names, Weary and Hoare, vivid in blue and gold over a white background; more amazed still to find Harold in a new suit, and seemingly in much better health than when he had left him.

'Well, you've properly bowled me over,' he admitted.

'I thought we were getting a bit stale,' replied Harold. 'I

want you to branch out a bit, Lionel. Don't be such a slave to the shop. I haven't been pulling my weight. Now I intend to.'

Miraculously, his health improved; and so a new phase opened in the history of Weary and Hoare which was soon remarked upon by everybody in the town. It was Mr Weary who now appeared more generally behind the counter; Mr Hoare who, quite often, was away on business. Their daily morning walk was continued, except during those week-ends when Mr Hoare had gone away. When he returned, it was always noticed that he was in exuberant spirits.

'Have a nice week-end?' the precentor would ask curiously.

'Oh, so-so! Just a little jaunt, y'know. Mustn't get rusty.'

'Where did you go?'

And from the other end of the counter would come Mr Weary's voice: 'You mustn't ask Mr Hoare questions like that, precentor.'

Lionel would laugh. 'That's right. Trade secrets, eh, Mr Weary?'

'And where *did* you go, Lionel?' Harold asked once, when they were alone in the kitchen.

'Never you mind, old man. That's a secret, like your poetry.'

No more reference was ever made to Lionel's week-ends.

With the jealous tenderness of an old lady to a cat did Harold Weary, during those last years of their life together, feed Lionel Hoare with his own subtle milk of human kindness. The fattening process continued well into the second year of the Second Great War. By that time Lionel had become very plump, his skin pink and patchy, his movements, once brisk and bird-like, now lethargic and sensuous. Harold, as though to compensate for his partner's weight, had wasted to a shadow, with a head shrunk deep into hunched shoulders. Many times Lionel had tried to induce him to get medical advice on his condition; but he never succeeded. After a time he gave it up and sleepily abandoned himself to bask and purr under the consumptive's ministrations. There were still the week-ends – at Bristol, Ilfracombe or Weston-super-Mare, and occasionally

London – when Lionel indulged his still amateur and long-delayed taste in women. Week-ends that remained an agreed secret – though Harold knew perfectly well to what foreign harbours his companion steered his dishonoured barque. But nothing must be said; Harold knew that. To pry into the other man's secret life would be to run the risk of losing him for ever.

So Lionel passed those lazy years, doing little in the shop or house, yet still responsible for the keeping of the accounts, and emerging into the shop at three to have a chat with the customers and talk of the old days and of Dr Rothway, now dead. So Harold, working with feverish energy, kept his friend fed, and at nights retired to his attic room to prune and ponder over those poems which nobody had ever seen. Then Lionel would play the piano and sometimes sing songs of Roger Quilter and Arthur Somervell; until ten-thirty, when Harold would bring him his cup of Bourn-Vita and send him to bed – in winter with a bottle.

Apart from the tediousness of the black-out and the encouragement of many memories of an earlier conflict, the war affected them very little. They would discuss their old experiences in the army, then lapse into a long silence over the fire, where the milk simmered in the saucepan. Then, with a sigh, Lionel would turn to his book-keeping.

'We've made a clear profit of seven hundred this year,' he remarked, one October evening in 1940; and he wondered what was the use of the money. He went on: 'I had a letter from the old man. He's very shaky now, and they've had some bombs up there. I ought to go and see him; it may be the last time. What're you looking at me like that for?'

Harold started. 'I didn't know I was looking at you. Sorry. Yes, I suppose you should go. How long?'

'It depends. We could close shop for a bit. Why don't you come too?'

'I don't want to. When will you go?'

'Tomorrow – or the next day – '

'Tomorrow?' Harold got up and started to make the Bourn-Vita. He was thinking of an interview he had had that morn-

ing with a doctor, an interview Lionel knew nothing about.
The doctor had given him three months of life, unless he were
prepared to go into a sanatorium in the Cheddar Hills. Even
then there was hope of little more. Harold did not fear death;
he welcomed it as a mistress he had wooed all his life, to whom
those heart-burning odes of his muse had been addressed. But
he feared for the future security and happiness of his friend.

'Can't you wait a month or so?' he asked.

'Better go before the winter sets in. You know how cold it
gets up there.'

'Tomorrow, then?' Harold spoke very quietly.

'I think so, Harold.'

'Well, go to bed now. You'll have a long day travelling.'

'I don't want to go to bed. I'd like to talk, Harold, about you
and me – and the queer mystery of our lives.'

Harold did not answer. Lionel was possessed of a desire to
tell him about Ilona, enjoyed a score of times in the women of
his week-ends. But he knew that Harold could never understand. Sadly he went to the stairs. 'I ought to be putting you to
bed,' he said. 'You're ill. Not me.'

'There's nothing wrong with me.'

'Except – '

'Except nothing. Here, take your Bourn-Vita.'

Lionel took the cup. 'I don't know,' he said, 'what power it
is you've got over me.'

'Power?'

'Yes. You always had. You know it.'

'You imagine it. You do as you like, don't you? You're
free?'

'No. I'm not free. I never shall be. Neither will you.'

He went to bed. For a long time Harold stared at the fire.
Yes, he thought, he had power all right; and how frightful that
power would be after death! Even now he began to relish the
prospect of the future when, unfettered by mortal chains, he
would be able, for the rest of Lionel's life, to stay by his side
– whispering in his ear, accompanying him upon his lonely
walks, attendant upon him during those sordid week-ends –

what limitless opportunities stretched before him! And all this – was he to throw it away at the command of some absurd altruism? At the end of the year, when January dawned, stark and cold, he would be free to haunt. 'No! No!' he cried. And all his genuine attachment to so old a friend rose up in him. At all costs he must be saved that fate. 'Kinder to kill than to haunt,' he muttered. And he remembered the decision he had made years ago.

Long into the night he sat there. The fire died out. Towards dawn he took a torch, went upstairs, listened outside Lionel's room, silently opened the door and crept to the bedside.

Cherubic and innocent, with a smile round the lips, Lionel lay in sleep. On the bedside table was the novel he had been reading, open at a page. By the light of the torch, Harold read: 'She drew him to her. All his tired manhood was enfolded and consecrated in the warmth of her bosom.'

Harold looked down at him. The time had come. His hands curled over the sleeper's throat, an inch away from the pink flesh. Then suddenly, with a little groan, he turned, tiptoed from the room, and closed the door. He could not do it. Lionel must take what had to come to him.

Lionel left for Yorkshire the following morning. He had the greatest misgiving about Harold as he stood in the corridor waving good-bye to him. The hectic rose-coloured spots on the white cheek-bones, the wasted body, the cold hand-clasp, the over-zealous dark eyes burning with an inner light, the husky voice and the strained breathing – all this gave to Harold Weary a melancholy nobility which remained fixed in Lionel's memory as the train drew out of the station. 'Perhaps it is the last time I shall see him,' he thought. Then he shuddered. Already he felt haunted. And a heavy feeling of guilt hung over him. His very health – his plumpness, his rich, rolling blue eye, his portly swagger, mild organist's hands – all this was a reproach to him when he thought of the emaciated figure in the black overcoat with the questing fire of the eyes of Don Juan awaiting necrophilous pleasures. 'I'll never go back,' he told himself. 'I'll give him my interest in the business.' But he knew, with a horrible certainty, that he would go back.

For five days Harold waited, hoping for word from Lionel that he was on his way home. On the fifth evening, when he had closed shop, he took the account books into the kitchen, counted the money in the till, and thought he had better make some effort to enter up the day-book. Always bad at figures, he found now that even to calculate the simplest sum was a task beyond him. He sat in the kitchen, over the ashes of a dead fire, groaning at the bitterness of his fate and cursing his life.

The door to the shop was open and a draught of wind cut through. But he was beyond feeling cold, for his heart was numbed, the passion of his life dead as the ashes in the grate. There was, he knew, but one gate left to happiness – and that gate, death, so soon to be opened, perhaps this night. Then might he hover forever over the life which had for twenty years been given to him and which he had nursed so single-mindedly. The whole pattern of his days was clear before him. An unfortunate soul, born to haunt, yet blessed beyond price in that he had found a host for his ghost. 'Thank God,' he muttered, 'I didn't kill him. Thank God I had the courage to wait.' He began, with pleasure, to contemplate the future. In what place, at what time, after his death, should he make his presence known to Lionel? He must do his best not to frighten him. Should he merely whisper in his ear in the night: 'Lionel! Guess who's here!' Or brush his cheek with a feather? Or announce himself by the sudden opening of a door as was the common way with so-called 'departed' spirits? None of these preliminary signs satisfied him. And there must certainly be no cheap poltergeist horseplay. There must be another way, some absolutely original way, for a ghost to make his first mark upon the page of the life he had lived.

Then he had it. In verse, in his own verse, should the hint be dropped. A page at a time, left casually on the table at night Terrifying? Probably. Yet the nature of the verses should compensate the haunted man for the chilled terror he would have to endure. For Lionel had always been desperately anxious to read his poetry.

Fired by this plan, Harold ran up to the attic to find the pages of a canto (it was an ode to Hecate) he had recently been purifying. Coming out from the attic, he paused on the landing. He had heard from far below, in the shop, two things: the ringing of the telephone, the playing of the piano.

For a moment he could not move. Then, dropping some of his manuscript on the stairs, he ran quickly down, calling out in a gasping voice, 'Who's there?'

He stumbled through into the dark shop. In God's name, what was that music, that wild, sweet melancholy from the upright Bechstein in the shop window, just behind the door? He knew it so well; he had heard it so many times.

The telephone still rang. Crashing into the cash-desk, he snatched the receiver. There was a telegram for Weary. He waited, the music still surging on in great passionate waves, like a ship lost in a huge sea and a black night. The voice came from the 'phone. 'My son killed in an air-raid last night. Writing.'

Then he knew who was playing the 'Valse Triste' on the Bechstein behind the door.

Outrage defeated terror, and he stumbled forward in the half-darkness of the shop. There was no figure seated before the piano; yet still the music continued. 'Stop that playing!' he screamed. Then he was convulsed by a fit of coughing.

Against the closing bars of the music a voice sounded: 'Half a mo, old man. If we're going to argue, might as well wait till I've finished.'

It was Lionel's voice, soft and warm, sounding from a dense pocket in mid-air. Then came the last three high chords of Sibelius's 'Valse' fading into the thin, cold whine of wind which rustled a pile of music on the counter. Then an unendurable silence and Harold knew that to be outraged was futile. Lionel had beaten him to the post.

'I'm sorry,' muttered Harold. 'You scared me, Lionel.'

'I meant to. Jolly well done, eh? What you might call a good sense of drama.'

'Where are you? Can you – appear?'

'I'm not saying what I can do.'

'That means you don't know how to.' Harold laughed bitterly. 'If only it were me – my God, how you'd suffer!'

'Yes. You wanted me to suffer, didn't you, old man?'

'On the contrary, I did my best – '

He was rudely interrupted by a copy of Mozart's Sonatas, which came whizzing through the air and fell at his feet.

'That's just to show you I know how to handle things over here. But don't worry. I'm going to look after you, with the same loving care you showed me.'

'Cheap tricks,' snapped Harold. 'Which any ghost could – '

'Get back to the kitchen.' The command shot out from somewhere in the cash-desk. 'You're standing in a direct draught and it's bad for you. You don't want to die yet.'

'You mean you don't want me to.'

There was a sudden push in Harold's back and he found himself in the kitchen. Again the voice came, apparently from the tea-pot.

'Poor Harold – struggling with the books – and the fire out! Lost without me, aren't you?'

'Not in the least.'

'Speak honest. What's the use of lying now? Light the gas-stove and put the milk on. You look worn out.'

'Why should I obey you?'

'Quite right. Why should you?'

There was a long silence. Then Harold broke it. 'Where are you? Why don't you speak?'

No answer. Harold laughed. It was clear that Lionel had declared a war of nerves. Challenged, he felt equal to it. Going upstairs, he opened the door of his attic. A voice chuckled from the desk. 'Well, Harold! I'd never have guessed! These poems of yours are quite hot stuff. Fancy you writing – '

'Leave my poems alone!' shrieked Harold. 'I won't have them touched by your filthy hands.'

'You mustn't, Harold, you really *mustn't*.' Lionel's voice purred, like a great cat, in his ear; a gloved hand touched his cheek.

'Don't touch me, either!' screamed Harold.

'I was wearing gloves when the bomb hit the Bradford train,' said Lionel. 'So you needn't worry, old man. My filthy hands won't touch you.'

'I didn't mean that. I'm sorry.'

'So am I. Since we've got to go on living together, Harold, we might as well make the best of it.'

'I shan't live long. You know that.'

'It doesn't make any difference whether you live or die. You can't escape me.'

'When I'm dead, you won't be able to escape me.'

There was no response to this. Harold sneered. 'That's got you. You never thought of that, did you?'

The curtains fluttered. There was silence. Harold sat the whole night in the attic, crouched over a miserable oil-stove. Except for the wild autumnal wind, the house was silent.

Perhaps it was, of all things, the long silences which were the most paralysing torments endured by the yet stoical personality of Mr Weary during his last few weeks on this earth. Stoical he certainly remained, betraying little of his trouble to those who came to the shop to offer their condolences on the death of his partner. The precentor, who now had a living at Wrothesbury Magna, cycled over a day after he had heard of the tragedy.

'My dear Weary, this is a dreadful blow to us all.'

Harold threw his leaf-like right hand into the air as though to offer his soul to whatever gods there be.

'Soon or late, death strikes,' he murmured.

The vicar hemmed, wondering whether to offer Christian consolation. He had heard that Weary was a subscriber to the Rationalist Press.

'There is every reason for a belief in the doctrine of Purgatory, my dear fellow,' he ventured. He had grown daringly

Anglo-Catholic since reaching the stall of Wrothesbury Magna.

'Purgatory,' remarked Harold, 'is perhaps nearer than we think.'

Lionel suddenly hissed from under the counter: 'So is Hell. Tell him that and see how he takes it.'

The vicar started. 'Did you say anything, dear fellow?'

'Nothing, vicar.'

The vicar sighed, intimated that he would say a mass for so dear a departed soul, and free-wheeled his cycle down Calverley Hill. It was near to Advent and he wanted to hear Steggall's anthem, 'Remember Now Thy Creator', sung in the cathedral. Advent came, with the wind shrieking in the stripped elms, and the élite of Calverley Hill staggering home under umbrellas that were almost wrested from their hands. They would hurry past Weary and Hoare's, noticing inside, under the warm pool of light over the counter, the drawn, predatory shape of Mr Weary, packing music back into the portfolios, then coming outside to draw the shutters. He closed early now, for there was seldom anyone to visit the shop after four-thirty. The old gatherings, which had once made the place merry with gossip, had ceased.

'You can't get much out of old Weary. Wonder what he thinks about every evening up there, alone? He plays the piano, anyway. I heard it as I passed the other night. Piano? But Weary never played the piano in his life. Hoare was the one who played. Queer! Oh well, I expect I imagined it.'

Every evening there alone … and how he longed to be alone! Yet he never saw his tormentor; always it was the voice, sounding from a place where he had least expected it. Once, after a long period of silence (it had been a week-end), he prophesied to himself, 'In five minutes his voice will sound from the coal-scuttle.' But quarter-of-an-hour elapsed before the voice came, from behind the reproduction of Lord Leighton's 'Wedded'. 'Funny you and I ever admitted a picture like this to the house, Harold, don't you think?'

Then Lionel would pester him to administer to himself various comforts, such as another cushion behind his head, more coal on the fire, what about a cup of tea, old long-face? He effectively bullied him into gathering all the windfalls from the orchard and storing them carefully in the attic. After that, Harold never wrote again. The over-heavy scent of decayed Blenheims made him feel sick. Lionel took exception to this.

'You can write in the kitchen, can't you?'

'I shall never write any more.'

'With a gift like yours, too! I've learnt quite a lot by heart. Listen!' So, for hours on end, Harold would be forced to listen to his own verses. At first he enjoyed this. Later, towards Christmas, the monotony of his heavy, mechanical iambics became an agony that was bitter to endure.

Then came the nightmare of Christmas, with Lionel making endless cracks about Mr Scrooge and hammering out all the most hackneyed carols on the piano. It was the end of Harold. On Boxing Day he could not leave his bed. Weak from lack of food, consumed by the fire of the disease, he abandoned himself to the hands of providence. There was no further fight left in him. When, on the day after Boxing Day, the shop did not open, a kindly neighbour who had for some time been anxious about him, knocked on the door. After a long wait Harold unbolted it and stared with blazing yet sightless eyes before him, down the long windy hill.

'Leave me alone,' he said, assuming that Lionel had knocked.

The neighbour stared at him. 'I'm so sorry – I thought you must be ill and in need of help, Mr Weary, and – '

'You know I'm joining you in a day or so. Can't you let me die in peace?'

The door was slammed. The neighbour ran, frightened, back to his own house, there to phone a doctor.

Very slowly Harold wandered up and down the shop. For two days there had been no visitation; and now, like one living in a country of gales, whose nerves are frayed when a day of calmness comes, he longed to hear Lionel's voice.

'Weary,' he muttered, 'Weary – you lived up to your name.'

And a voice hummed in his ear, 'Art thou languid?'

He smiled. He was almost at peace. 'No. I'm weary,' he whispered. Then he struggled upstairs to his bed, where he lay stretched out on the disordered clothes, half hearing from the still blacked-out window the reluctant sounds of men and women about their normal work after the Christmas break.

At mid-day the doctor came. Knocking brought no answer, neither did shouts up to the window. The door had to be forced. They found Harold alive, but barely conscious. A district nurse was summoned and bade to stay with him for the night. It could only be a question of a few hours, the doctor said. There was no point in removing the patient to an already overcrowded hospital.

It was the middle of the night when the nurse woke from a half-sleep. She had heard a cry. Harold was sitting up in bed, his arms extended, an expression of longing on his face. 'Yes,' he managed to gasp, 'yes – we did it – somehow we did it – somehow we escaped ...'

The nurse held him. But with the strength of a dying man he pushed her aside. In his ears was Lionel's voice.

'I've been wandering through the shop, Harold, looking my last at it all. I shan't come here again. You're going, and there's nothing for me to come back for, except, perhaps, to have a tune on the Bechstein sometimes. I think it's a good little place, Harold. We made something, you and I, neither of us could have made alone. Men wouldn't have remembered Weary; nor would they have remembered Hoare. But Weary and Hoare – ay, lad, they'll remember Weary and Hoare. You and me – we're nothing – never could be. I'm not even a ghost – only your imagination – that's all. We pass out like leaves – like leaves, old man. We've escaped into two names which people will remember. Weary and Hoare.'

'Ay!' Harold's deep great eyes stared before him. His voice came quieter than mist over the sea. 'Weary and Hoare – Weary and Hoare – '

The head fell forward. The nurse, having performed her merciful tasks, rinsed her hands and went down to phone the doctor. In the cash-desk she hesitated, her head turned towards the shop. She thought she had heard the sound of a piano.

No will being found, the property passed to a second cousin of Mr Weary who, a year later, answered the solicitor's advertisement. Obtaining the keys of the shop, he went in there, one fine spring day of 1942.

Nothing had been touched. There were the neat piles of music, the busts of Mozart, Bach, Beethoven, on top of the high shelves, and dust thick as flour on everything. Something lay on the floor. The visitor picked it up – a copy of Mozart's Sonatas. It was so thick with dust, he dropped it in disgust, and wiped his fingers on his overcoat.

He went all over the house. In the attic he glanced for a moment at the rotten apples and the heap of charred papers in the grate. Picking up one half-burnt sheet, he read a few lines of poetry. It did not interest him. Going downstairs, he took one last look at the shop, then padlocked the door and returned to the solicitor. He left instructions to sell the place, lock, stock and barrel.

But a buyer could not be found, and nobody ever cared to take the peeling shutters down from the windows, or, as people will, to pry into the premises.

For the 'Valse Triste' is still heard from the piano on the other side of that door where dead leaves, mingling with the tattered leaves of music which have slipped through from the darkened shop, rustle and crackle in the wind.

V

The Chocolate Box

Intense repugnance. That is one definition of horror to be found in the dictionary. Or, *power of exciting such feeling.*

I think it is more. It is also what is totally unexpected: the long sunlit lane that has only a brick wall at the end, the worm in the rose, the sudden ravaged image of one's own tormented face in a window pane. That which has sudden power to corrupt and defile. A stench where sweetness should be; darkness where light should be; a grin where a smile should be; a scream searing into a night where silence should be. An old withered hand where a young hand should be ...

And no escape from whatever it may be that has suddenly come upon the visitant. No escape.

I write those words by way of preface to the story of something that happened to me fifty years ago. And immediately I ask myself whether I want to tell the story, or *why* I have to tell it. I must. That is all. If only because – but let the reason come later.

It does not seem possible that it was fifty years ago, and I – a young man living alone in a mine-pitted valley near Land's End where on nights of no moon the darkness had a surging, living quality in which I could hear not only the waves of the sea but the waves of the music I knew I would write; a young man with great ambitions that have only been sparely fulfilled. With my music – scores of composers then considered avant-garde, such as Stravinsky, Schoenberg, Hindemith – and a few books and a stack of virgin scorepaper, I had rented a cottage in this remote valley, barely furnished, but containing all I needed except one thing – a piano. And the arrival of this, my old black Bord, I awaited from London. Against the advice of parents and friends I had come as far west as I could go, there to come to terms with the music I knew I must compose. Nothing else mattered.

But this is not a story about music. I must keep it out, otherwise it will flood the pages and consume me. I am writing of a particular night in spring, a night of pitch darkness when I was walking down the valley to my retreat, after an evening in the King's Arms.

Let me get it as clearly and simply as I can. Without comment, and no 'ornaments' to use a musical term I like. Bleak, as it was. Very bare.

Half way down the valley, along a path treacherous with jagged stones and lichenous boulders, I drew up sharply. I could not see, but I knew someone was coming up the same path towards me. I stopped. The other person stopped too. A moment of silence, then I could hear his breathing – for I knew somehow it was a man. He came closer, and I drew aside.

'Good-night, Mister.'

I heard the words, husky and defensive. And almost before I could return his greeting he had passed me, and I could hear his footsteps, getting dimmer, crunching over little stones. I had no idea who he was, nor did it much trouble me, after the first shock. I had had too good an evening at the King's Arms, I was too full of imagined music – a theme in B minor played in my head, with a recurring B, reminiscent of the 'raindrop' Prelude of Chopin – and its supporting harmony, possible weaving of counterpoint, was beginning to form in my mind. So I went on, and in a few moments the stranger had left my mind.

Perhaps thirty steps on I stopped again. My foot had touched an object in the path, and it was not a stone. Something soft, something I felt should not be there. You must understand that there was nothing in the least frightening about this. I was far too full of music to be frightened of anything. But I stopped none the less, struck a match, and bent down, shielding the flame from the slight breeze blowing from the sea – a western breeze that smelt of rain. Already I could smell the sweetbriar from the steep hillside garden of my cottage. And the B minor theme drifted into the major. (Keep music out – oh, keep music out. It has nothing to do with what I am trying to relate....)

In the light of the match I saw what seemed and was incongruous in that setting. A chocolate box, a familiar box of those times, one with a picture of King George V on it, and crossed by a red ribbon. A white cardboard box. A pound box. I laughed. It seemed absurd, lying there. It was familiar to me, because these were the chocolates my mother liked best. We had always had them at home, they belonged to my childhood. What was it doing here? I could swear for certain it had not been there earlier in the evening, when I had walked up the valley.

Obviously, I told myself, it would be empty. And yet I had to pick it up, to be sure, even though I was not in a chocolate-eating frame of mind that night, having drunk many pints of beer (fourpence a pint in those days). So I did pick it up, and realized at once that it was not empty. The match went out, and it was the last in the box. So on I went in the enfolding darkness, holding the box, vaguely wondering if it contained chocolates, and remembering a melody by Dvorak, 'Songs my Mother taught me'.

Inside the cottage I found another box of matches, lit the lamp, then the small Beatrice oil-stove, and put a kettle on for tea. The room became warm and welcoming in the glow of the lamp which lit up score paper littered over the table. I longed for the piano. It was a night when I wanted to improvise, to hear those sounds which played in my mind. Yet I was content to wait. The piano would come in the course of the next few days. Putting the chocolate box down on the table, I cut a hunk of bread and found some cheese. The silence of the night was broken only by the trickling stream deep in the valley. And in this sound my B major theme evolved into a new episode.

I remember that I did not hurry anything. There is a kind of happiness, almost an ecstasy, which can flow into the soul when it is least expected. And this is what filled me then, coupled with the assurance that very soon with my piano I would begin to hear the music I was hearing now only in my mind.

I made the tea, ate some bread and cheese, lit a cigarette, and then looked again at the chocolate box which still lay on the table. It was damp from the night air, slightly browned. But it was, it seemed to me, friendly – like a message from home which said, 'Don't worry, you are on the right path.' I was reluctant to open it, and even wondered whether I would do so that night.

But at last – and by now it was well past midnight – I did open it. At once, I drew back a little. I saw something wrapped in tissue paper, something stained a sullen rusty red. And like a flash of lightning the whole scene changed, the whole peaceful contented mood was shattered. Whatever was wrapped in that tissue paper I knew that I did not want to take it out and examine it. Yet I had to do so.

As I looked down at the object wrapped in the tissue paper a new sound came insistently into my ears. I tried to ignore this sound. I tried to gather back into my mind the music which, only a few minutes earlier, had been moving there, making its own form and order. But it would not return. I only knew the key: B minor. And could only hear this new sound – a humming, a buzzing, which rose to a crescendo, then sank to a diminuendo until it died away completely, leaving only the sound of the stream outside.

And still I was staring down at the open box.

I put my hand down to touch the tissue paper, then drew back. The sound had come again, and this time nearer, then broken by a strange blundering little thud, which should have finished it, yet did not. For now the sound was close to my ear. Something brushed my face and I put my hand up involuntarily, slapping my cheek.

It was a bluebottle. I saw it veer drunkenly above the lamplight, then swoop down in an arc towards the box, then away again.

I tried to laugh. Bluebottles are loathsome, I have always

hated them. But to be almost panic-stricken by one was clearly absurd. And as to what was wrapped in the tissue paper . . .

I took it out, and drew back a little of the paper. I saw what looked like the nail of a finger – a blackened nail, horny and scored with yellow cracks.

The bluebottle swooped down. Suddenly I shouted at it, and at the same moment drew away the folds of paper from the object in my hand.

In my hand . . . There it was. A hand in a hand. A dead hand cradled in a living hand. A left hand, severed at the wrist, hacked away and still bleeding.

I laid it down, then drew back with a hiss. I felt sick. From a fold in the window curtain, drawn towards the hand like steel to a magnet, the bluebottle loomed across the room. It settled where it wanted to settle. On the dead hand.

My mouth was open, as though to release something foul inside me. I could do nothing for several seconds but stare down at the hand and the bluebottle stalking across the palm with its broken-up lines and branches. Then I looked away to the bright circle of red light from the little oil cooker – always a comforting glow. It was late April, and the air was clammy and heavy after a day of heavy showers. There was no sound now from the bluebottle. The silence seemed to solidify, I felt as though the bracken-breasted hills each side of the valley were meeting and closing in upon me. There was a faint satisfied humming again, as the insect delved deeper into the palm of the severed hand. I forced myself to look at it.

It was not a large hand. Wrinkled, with long fingers and black grimy nails, unfreckled, hairless. I put down my own hand as though to touch it, but could not. Still, in a half bemused manner, I could not quite believe it was there – the thing that should not be there.

I blew on it, which disturbed the bluebottle and sent him crashing crazily round the room, angry, defiant.

It wasn't true, I told myself. It could not be true. If I had had a piano here I could have beaten back the rising sickness in me. As it was, I retched, went quickly out to the door, and was sick.

I stayed, wiping my mouth, looking into the solid darkness. Then I remembered the man who had passed me, muttering 'Good night, Mister', and so quickly disappeared. Who was he?

Getting control of myself, I returned to the cottage, half hoping, yet knowing it could not be, that the hand would not be there.

It was there. Calmly now, I put the lid back on the box, telling myself I must take it to the police station next morning.

I went up to bed. Whether it was the amount of beer I had drunk, I do not know. But, mercifully, I slept – for several hours. I awoke suddenly, before dawn – not with any memory of the hand, not out of some nightmare, but struggling to recall music which had drifted back into my sleeping mind. I sat up. If I could get downstairs now, I told myself, and touch the keyboard of a piano, the music would return.

But there was no piano downstairs. And suddenly I remembered what was there. Then, until the sun rose over the shoulder of the valley, I lay awake, remembering it was a spring morning when I should have been happy.

It is difficult to keep music out of this story I have to tell, and yet I must try. Try to relate the incongruous events quite simply, as though they had not happened to me, but to someone else; as though it were an account of something I might have read in a newspaper.

And when I write 'it is difficult to keep music out,' I mean simply that music – or the lack of it – played so large a part in the events of the following days, days in which I tried so desperately to recall the themes which had been in my mind before I opened that box. Themes which would not return, and now, perhaps, never will.

What happened, as I came downstairs the next morning, remembering what had been on the table, lying on top of the score paper, the night before? Nothing happened. I remembered the chocolate box as one remembers a dream, and still held on half desperately to the hope that it had been a dream.

But it had not. For there the box was, still on the table where I had left it; and my cup, the sugar basin, plate and knife, ashtray, books, lamp, papers. Everything was exactly as I had left it, including the opened box and what it contained.

There is a hard, matter-of-fact side to my nature, a ruthless side if you like, which can at times come to the rescue. It did then. Hardly looking at the hand, I put the lid on the box and took it over to the window seat, where I left it. It was quite straightforward, I said. Somebody had chosen to leave a severed hand in a chocolate box. I had had the misfortune to pick it up and bring it home. It must go to the police station. That was all there was to it. No concern of mine.

But a curious thing happened. As I put the box in the window seat it seemed to me that it had already become part of the place. I suppose I was trying to rationalise the matter. I had found something, brought it home; and here it was. Why should it be any more offensive than, say, a stone from the beach, a spray of blackthorn, or wreckwood washed up in Priest's Cove – things which, in fact, I had found, and were now in the room? Things which had become part of me, part of my life.

So, with this box, and its content. Perhaps it had been dropped by the man who had passed me in the night. But I had found it, I had brought it back. 'Findings keepings,' I muttered, and found myself laughing – laughing, I now know, to keep fear at bay.

So I opened the box again, and again with the half thought that I might have only dreamt, or seen in a drunken haze, what had been there last night. But there was no escape from it. The hand was still there.

Without touching it (this I could not yet bring myself to do) I looked at it closely, quite dispassionately. The bleeding had stopped. A thick coagulation of dried blood had sealed the carpal bones at the wrist. I thought it had changed a little during the night; the colour was different, slightly greenish. Living, what had the hand done? Written letters, caressed lovers, held a spade, slid forefinger and thumb into scissors, struck blows, waved aside the sea as the body swam, picked flowers, played a piano —

It was then that I put the lid on the box and tried, oh so hard, tried to forget it.

I make these breaks in the story because as I write, I falter — trying to remember; and because I write with pain and a sense of loss I cannot overcome. And once again I tell myself — I must try to stick to the facts. What happened that day?

I suppose I made breakfast — coffee, toast, marmalade, and plenty of the rich dark yellow butter which you could buy then in pound slabs from the farm above the valley. I may have read a little from the local paper, for I liked to pretend to myself that I was concerned to some extent with events around me. I wanted to feel that I was a citizen in this unknown western country, that I would be accepted as 'one of them,' that a man who had decided to spend his life composing music which perhaps nobody would want to hear had his right place in the world.

But whatever I did, as I sat in that room, every now and again I would look across to the window seat, half hoping that the box would not be there, and yet — in a most curious way — calmed when I saw that it was. I cannot describe adequately, or understand, this new sense of ownership that was stealing into me. As though I had found treasure and was already hoarding it.

I remember that I had planned that day to break in a triangle of land up the slope behind the cottage, where I intended to put down some gladiolus bulbs. And I refused to allow the hand to alter my plans, particularly as the sun was now fully risen into a clear sky. It would be absurd to put off what I had intended to do on so lovely a spring day.

And so I worked on the hillside, well into the late afternoon, only coming in for some bread and cheese about noon. From time to time, as I dug into the rough ground I found myself muttering 'the Hand, the Hand,' already giving it the honour of a capital letter. Hand. And I would look at my own hands at the spade, thinking — this isn't the kind of work these hands are meant to do. I need to use my fingers – at the piano. Then I would dismiss these thoughts, and go on digging, beginning to hate the earth.

I remember suddenly hearing the call of a cuckoo, very near to me, near enough to startle, and realizing that there is only enchantment in this creature's falling major third (and later, minor) when he is heard from a distance. But when he is near, then the falling notes are like blows on the ear; and you remember that the bird is like a pirate. Delius would not have written his idyllic piece for orchestra had he heard the cuckoo as I heard him that day.

By six o'clock, rain had started to fall. Clearly it was blowing up for a souwester. It was always the wind I loved, and I love it still, but that evening, as the sun went down and the valley darkened and the wind began to rush in great gusts from the sea, I did not love it. I had intended walking up to the village in the evening, taking what I had found to the police station, then to the King's Arms, to drink and try to forget the whole matter –

Try to forget it! As though that were possible. And it was not the kind of evening in which to take the long trek to the village; for now the rain was driving in slanting sheets, filling the gushing stream in the valley. It was one of those evenings in late spring when winter makes a sudden dramatic reappearance and you long for darkness to come. But darkness is delayed, and the heart grows cold as you look at the empty grate, choked up with old cigarette packets – Player's, at sixpence for ten. Light a fire, I said. Go out to the shed and bring in some driftwood. But when I opened the door, the force of the wind almost knocked me back. I shut it fiercely, drew the curtain across the doorway to the small living-room, sat down, and clenched my fists, looking at them. There were blisters at the base of the fingers of my right hand. Were there blisters on –

The Hand possessed me. I tried to read – Rimsky-Korsakov on orchestration. But the words made no sense, and a torrent of chaotic music in my mind made me want to scream. The piano – why wasn't there a piano? That could have saved me.

Save me? From what? For I am still alive to tell the tale. But I mean, a piano could have saved me from the inner darkness and rising void which like its sister darkness in the valley outside the cottage walls rose up as though to suffocate me. I did not read or even know the name of Gerard Manley Hopkins in those days; he had hardly emerged upon the literary scene. But now I can quote from him, in illustration of my condition then.

O the mind, mind has mountains; cliffs of fall
Frightful, sheer, no-man-fathomed.

(And this from the poet who died unknown, with none of his verses published, and on his lips the last words, 'I am so happy.')

Yes, the piano would have saved me, or any sound of music. But in particular I would then have played from the Well-Tempered Clavichord, for in Bach I could have found the strength, the consolation, the perfect *order* without which art and life have no meaning.

But there was no piano. And as the window panes misted with heat from the oil stove and the driving rain hissed and bubbled down the gutters I could think only of one thing: the box in the window seat. What had stopped me from going straight up to the village and handing it over to the police? Merely the drenching rain? No, it was more than that, or so my sick conscience seemed to tell me. I was afraid to become involved. There would be questions I would not be able to answer. Would my story even be believed – that I had merely stumbled upon the box in the dark? But worse than that, my conscience drove at me the awareness that in some dreadful way I could not explain to myself, *I did not want to part with it.* As that long black evening drew on to night, and midnight, and past midnight, and still I did not go up to bed, and had by now smoked the last cigarette, I knew that this was the real reason why I had rejected the long walk to the village.

It had fallen in my path. It was mine. I wanted to keep it.

I can remember now a moment of wild humour that rose in me, when I spoke aloud, trying to reassure myself. 'Bloody fool. What is it? Nothing but a Hand in a chocolate box. People are constantly leaving hands in chocolate boxes and dropping them on remote paths in west Cornwall.' And it was with a laugh of sheer bravado that at last I went to the box, and once again lifted its lid.

A thought came to me as I looked down. The box was packed with power. I bent down to take a closer look at it. And as I did so, I heard the sound I had subconsciously expected, yet had, at this moment, forgotten about.

It came from a corner of the room I could not place. Or did it come from the floor, from the tattered oil-stained rush matting before the slab, the rusty slab which had not been lit for so long? Or did it come from inside myself?

At first, I would not let this sound worry me. I felt calm, as though I were no more than a pawn in a game of chess, and must move as I was moved. So I merely looked and looked down at the Hand. Again, it seemed to have changed. Was it true that nails grow after death? I did not know, but I believe now that they do. And here, certainly, on these dead cold sticks of half curled fingers, the nails were longer, crustier, than they had been the last time I had looked.

Gnarled, tobacco-stained ... and now the colour had a purplish-greeny glow. In the centre of the palm I could see a thick black moving spot.

It was when I saw the spot that the sound stopped. It was the bluebottle. It had settled precisely where it had wanted to settle.

Not until that moment did I lose control. The next second I was looking through misted eyes at the shattered bits of a cup I had thrown across the room. It had crashed into a mirror on the wall by the door, a small oval mirror framed in an absurd fretsaw design of little crosses. The glass was splintered, and the bits of china scattered over the table. Tea had spilled across a sheet of score paper on which I had written the beginning of a subject – a dribble of quavers.

That was the moment when I cried out the name of Christ, and snatching up the score papers, tore them in two, and then tore again, and again, and set a match to them, and watched them burn. That was the moment when I threw away the work I had meant to do, the work I was meant to do, and the moment when I consented to evil.

And then I was calm again. Putting the lid back on the box, I went upstairs to bed. I slept. And that night I was not disturbed by any dreams of music.

'The moment when I consented to evil . . .'

It is too great a condemnation; I know that. And yet, from that moment I can now see my life as a composer was ended. What threads I have taken up have not been the right ones. And if I compose now, or play now, the sounds are not in good order.

I must finish this account of something that happened to me so long ago, which I would never have written had it not been for a letter I received recently from an old friend who lives still in that part of Cornwall – a letter I will quote from presently.

The stormy weather continued well into the following day. But by some intuition I knew it would end before evening, I knew the sun would break through the mass of cloud as the day wore on. I cannot remember now what I did with the earlier part of that day – whether I once opened the box or not. I only remember that at about six o'clock a glow of watery sun suddenly came across the opposite hillside, and again I heard the cuckoo, this time far away, yet not soothing, not on notes of ecstasy. It was to be a clear night. A night when one sees the slip of a new moon. I now had to do what should have been done twenty-four hours earlier, or even before that. I had to go to the village and give up to the police what I had only just found two nights before. I would tell them, I decided, that I had only just found it. For what kind of questions would I be asked if I admitted that I had kept it for nearly two days?

I am trying to remember each move I made that evening. I think it was like this. I would have to return a milk jug and a

cream bowl to the farm at the top, and these I put in a haversack. Bread had to be collected from the farm on the way
back, where it was left for me twice a week. Probably it was
a Saturday night, when, in those days, shops stayed open late.
I intended to buy stores for the next few days, and that must
have been why I took the haversack.

The last thing I did was to take the box from the window
seat, outside, and there I rested it on a stone hedge, while I put
the milk jug and cream bowl into a haversack. I remember that
moment well. For the thought came to me (and why did I not
follow it up?) that I should bury the Hand; bury it and forget
it. Even give it a little funeral service as they did in the superb
tale of Maupassant, the tale of the fisherman's hand that had
become gangrenous. Yes. I should have done that. It would
have been kinder.

Instead ... and it was not until I got to the farm that I realized what I had done. Taking the haversack from my shoulders in order to leave the jug and cream bowl with Mrs Harry
I stared at her in a way that must have frightened her.

'It's nothing,' I said, in answer to her question. 'Something I
meant to take to the village. That's all.'

'Tesn't the end of the world,' she said.

No. I agreed. It was not the end of the world. And I went
up to the village, did my shopping, and spent the rest of the
evening in the King's Arms. I had left the chocolate box on the
stone hedge outside the cottage.

Why did I not go back for it? And what would have happened
had I done so? Would it still have been there, on the stone
hedge, in its box where I had left it? Or would only the box
have been there, as it was when I returned late that night to the
cottage?

I kept asking these questions, as I have asked them many
times in the last fifty years – intermittently, it is true, trying to
bury the inexplicable, even to pretend that I had imagined it
all, from the beginning, that I had never even found the box
in my path. But it cannot be buried, any more than I can now

bury the Hand; and now, because of this letter I have had, and because of something else, it has had to be written – written out of me, I hope; written right out of my system.

I have not made it clear. Would only the box have been there, I have written above, had I gone back for it? By that I mean, when I did return late at night, only the box *was* there.

There was nothing inside it.

At first, as I stared down at the empty box in the light of my torch, and saw only dark brown stains, there was a sense of lightness in me, almost relief. It had gone. Perhaps it had never been there. The whole business the product of a disordered mind. But then I knew this was not so. The hand had been taken away. But who had taken it?

At what time, I asked myself, had I again met the man I had passed in the dark two nights earlier? At what time had I passed him that evening? And hardly noticed him?

Yes, it had been a few moments after I left the farm, continuing my walk into the village. An old man, wearing a long shabby grey overcoat that had once been good, an old man with a shuffling walk and furtive expression, an old man who did not show his hands, for they (if two there were) were in his coat pockets. He had passed me with a quick upward glance at me, and he had muttered something I hadn't heard. I had hurried past, not wanting to admit his presence even into my mind. But he had been walking down in the direction of the valley. And I have never seen him again, I never found out who he was.

I had spent an almost convivial evening in the King's Arms. I remember making jokes about hands to the landlord, old Bill Jago he was called. 'Hands,' I had said, 'funny things when you look at them. Think what they can do.' And he had looked at me a little oddly, wondering what I was talking about, and why I was so closely examining my own two hands laid palm upwards on the bar counter.

'Never thought much about them meself,' he said.

'Well, do,' I advised him. 'Because they're precious things. If you lost one, then you'd think about it.'

A crude, macabre joke, which I had enjoyed, perversely relishing the knowledge of what I thought still reposed in the
box on the stone hedge. No need to report this matter to the
police, I told myself. It had been taken out of my hands ...

At first, as I have said, I had this sense of lightness and relief,
when I found the empty box, and took it in, and looked again
and again at it. Tonight, the cottage was dead silent. The wind
had dropped. In the window seat I saw a dead bluebottle. Scattered all over the floor the charred bits of score paper. Then,
and not till then, did I begin to feel a dreadful sense of loss.
Even if it had been the hand of a killer, *I wanted it back.*

As I grow older, and my left hand hardens and becomes
more useless so that I begin to drop things from cramped and
bloodless fingers even on fine summer mornings, I feel how
much easier it could be if I had the Hand safely back in the
chocolate box. What would be left of it now? A writhing mess
of maggots? But no. That happened a long time ago. Or did it?
For here is a part of the letter I had from a friend recently, the
letter which made me write of this.

> ... Things don't change much in Penwith. Every now
> and again the odd, unaccountable event, the sort of thing
> Cornwall belongs to have. For example, the other day half
> in the stream at the bottom of the Kenidzhak Valley – wasn't
> that where you used to live? – the dead body of an old man
> was found. Nobody here seemed to know anything about
> him – he had no friends, no relatives. Somebody said, at the
> inquest, they thought he had once been a church organist.
> But it was all very vague. What *wasn't* vague, however, and
> what makes the story interesting – for you'll agree that the
> dead body of an old unknown person isn't all that arrest
> ing – was the fact that he had only one hand. His left hand
> had been cut off at the wrist – hacked off pretty crudely, the
> pathologist said, perhaps with a meat axe ...

This is the reason why I have had to write the story, for which
I will never be able to give any explanation. Nor do I really

want to. Thomas Mann wrote a masterpiece, *Death in Venice.* My 'death in Venice' it seems to me, happened in youth, a very long time ago. Of course I have made some use of my musical talent. I am well known as a critic; people read me in the papers – I have even dealt not inadequately with contemporary electronic music and come to terms with people like Stockhausen.

And sometimes I play the piano. Not well. Passably. To amuse myself. When I had my friend's letter I went to an old chest in which for years I have kept papers, music, books, press cuttings, photographs. I knew I still had it. And there it was. The chocolate box.

I look at it now as I write. Why did I keep it? I never put anything in it, and I suppose I kept it only as evidence of something that did really happen. What shall I use it for now? Or shall I at last burn it?

There is still a faint brown stain in it. And as I put the lid back and look again at the picture of George V and think of my mother and how she loved these particular chocolates, I hear something in the room. It is a humming, a buzzing, coming and going.

I do not think it will ever stop, this noise. It is always in my ears.

VI

Quintin Claribel

From his earliest infancy, Quintin Claribel had fallen victim to two tyrants: words, and his own tongue. The tongue was very ready to express in words thoughts that should have stayed in his mind, or sometimes thoughts that had never been in his mind until the words planted them there. The words themselves were sweeter tyrants, acknowledged and revered; it mattered not to the child what a word meant; had it a pleasant sound it demanded, sooner or later, the service of his tongue. Such words as 'orphrey, balm, tiercel, sponge, incest, loosestrife, vaseline' – these were music to his ears at even such an early age as eight.

Perhaps Miss Bond, who once told him that Lewis Carroll's poem Jabberwocky 'meant nothing,' was partly responsible; according to Quintin she was certainly responsible for his ultimate punishment. This lady, a firm character who always believed in saying what you meant – who, in fact, treated words merely as weights in the scales of wisdom – was his governess. The unique history of Quintin Claribel does undoubtedly begin in the schoolroom at Hassocks where daily he sat picking up stale crumbs of Miss Bond's scholarship.

'Have you,' she might ask, 'mastered the first declension yet, Quintin?'

She would not look at him as she asked the question. With her right forefinger she would trace designs in her left palm as though, in those lines of fate and head and heart she read, not her own future, but her pupil's. It was a trick that fascinated Quintin. Watching her, he would forget to answer, until again she would speak, her head still bent over the cupped palm, but the voice keener now, the words clipped shorter.

Then, hurriedly, he would reply: 'Oh yes, Miss Bond! Oh yes! I've learnt it.'

'Then repeat it!' And suddenly with this command, both Miss Bond's hands would come down slap on the desk and he would find himself gazing emptily at her rounded owl-like face.

'*Mensa, mensa* – ' Here Quintin might stammeringly pause.

'You have *not* mastered it!' Miss Bond would cry, almost with pleasure it seemed to Quintin. 'Why did you say that you had?'

'I didn't mean it, Miss Bond. I meant to say that I was just in the middle of learning it.'

'Would it not be better to say what you mean?'

Quintin could find no response to that. And because he was so often trapped by his governess, he came gradually to hate her. She was, for one thing, so ugly; so frighteningly like an owl. He was sure she hooted in the night and devoured mice in the small hours. Like an owl, the inscrutable face was expressionless. She knew everything; and he felt he would never know anything.

One bright frosty morning in early January, Quintin found it even more difficult than usual to keep his mind upon his studies. Miss Bond was standing with her back to the fire, pointing with a long rod to the position of Australia on the globe. Quintin was cold; Miss Bond looked very warm. If, the child wondered, he were to hold out his hands and warm them in front of her, would she take the hint and move a little?

His seat was near the window. His eyes strayed to the frosted walnut tree and beyond, to the park where, over a thin crust of snow, shaggy cattle moved. The pond would be frozen. Surely it was idle to sit here and consider Australia on such a morning, when a new pair of skates reposed on the shelf in his bedroom cupboard?

She was speaking.

'Be so good as to tell me, Quintin, what do we mainly import from Australia?'

He heard the question, asked for a second time, and in his

mind a swarm of words buzzed. Cotton, wool, coal, tea, coffee, candles, rice, copal, gum? Making a supreme effort, Quintin sought to clutch on to one of these words, hoping it would rescue him from this slough of uncertainty. 'Copal' was the word that seemed most likely, since he did not know what copal was, and invariably the right answer turned out to be only the prelude to further questions equally unanswerable. Quintin, if he understood nothing else, understood Miss Bond's technique. Were 'copal' to be the required word, she would at once pounce on him: 'And what is copal, may I ask?' Perhaps, then, it was wiser to grasp another word from his mental list. 'Tea' for example. But something told him that tea was not Australian; it was Chinese. Should he fling himself boldly into battle and announce that he knew what came from China? But his distaste for the word 'tea' (could it be called a word at all?) overcame this impulse.

Struggling thus to answer, he did indeed open his mouth intending to utter the word 'copal' – the best sounding word of the lot. But other words lay back in his mind, words that flavoured his mouth and made him want to curl up with joy. The word 'vile' for example. Shivering with the cold, sliding his hands between his stockinged knees, he opened his mouth very wide, certain now that he could answer Miss Bond. Instead of answering her, he gasped out the three dreadful words:

'Vile old owl!'

An ominous cloud surged into the pale face of the governess. Her wand clattered to the floor, lying like Aaron's rod on the rug before the fire, ready to writhe and hiss at Quintin in defence of its mistress.

After the first shock Miss Bond behaved with acid courtesy. The offence was grave indeed, but it must be met calmly and with fortitude.

'What – ' she spoke very quietly, ' – did I hear you say, Quintin?'

The three terrible words were ringing in his head. Could he possibly have spoken them? He looked round as though in search of another culprit. Somebody in that cupboard; somebody behind that screen; one of those Watteau-like vignettes that swung from peachy frills and tassels in the tapestry above the fireplace; the anvil jaw of Napoleon Buonaparte from his frame over the bookshelves. Could any of these have spoken? But no! It was too clear that his own tongue, that irresponsible instrument of his darkest thoughts, had made public what should have been forever private.

Suddenly Miss Bond spoke again, less calmly.

'What did I hear you say, Master Quintin?'

He burst up from his chair in distress.

'I didn't mean it, Miss Bond; really, I didn't. I was thinking of what you asked me. Copal, that's what I meant. I didn't mean it was you who was the vile old – '

'Enough!'

Miss Bond's hand shot up sharply, checking a repetition of the offensive word.

'I wonder,' she said (and there was sadness in her voice) for who knew better than herself that she was not beautiful?) 'that those wicked words don't freeze in the air as a perpetual reproach to you, Quintin.'

Walking to the window she turned her back upon him, perhaps to hide the unfortunate face that had prompted the outrageous words or perhaps to imprint the insult upon the ice-grey sky.

Again, desperately, Quintin tried to restore himself to her favour.

'Please, Miss Bond, I really didn't mean it. I don't know what made me say it. I wasn't thinking of you. I didn't mean it was you who was the vile – '

Again Miss Bond stopped him.

'One day,' she said, 'you will eat your words, Quintin.'

And with something like a sob, she turned and left the room. Had he called her a liar, a murderer, a thief – these she could have borne because they would have been so manifestly untrue. But to be called an owl – and a *vile* one, an *old* one – some ghastly truth lurked there. Hurrying to her bedroom she locked the door and surveyed herself in her mirror.

Alone, Quintin turned gloomily to the fire and warmed himself. Now that the thing had happened he wasn't really sorry. In the first place, surely it was true, what he had said? Truer than tea from Australia or copal from China. In the second place she had gone and now he could get warm.

But why stay by the fire? This was not the way to get warm on a winter morning.

Going to the door, he crept upstairs, ran to his bedroom, found his skates and came down. In another minute he was outside, running past the walnut tree, over the little bridge, to the park.

Soon, in a hollow in the land, the house was lost. The morning, the ice, his freedom stretched before him.

While he skated he found himself fascinated by the twirling spirals that he was making on the ice; in time, if he practised, he would be able to make figures, signs, words. Even wonders. The morning passed all too quickly. The stable clock chimed the three-quarters-to-one; he would have to return to an angered mother and father.

Unwillingly he took off his skates, slung them over his shoulder and stood moodily looking at the beautiful designs of his exercise. There, clear on the ice, was a great letter 'O'; so perfect a letter that he could not resist putting on his skates again, going to the ice and soaring up and down in angles, driven by a mad desire to engrave the letter 'W' on the pond. He came back to the grass and surveyed what he had made. Not a very good 'W.' 'OW,' he said. And then stopped. 'OW?' But surely? Yes – and so she was A *vile* old owl. He bit his lip. But she was!

Very slowly he walked up the rising field towards the house. By now the sky was heavy with fresh snow. He stopped for a moment on the bridge. It was very quiet. A few flakes of snow fell. It seemed as though everything had lost its voice so that the patter of the snow upon the ground could be clearly heard. For the last time, aware that he must never utter them aloud again, Quintin, in the silence, spoke clearly and happily the three words that had given him a morning on the ice.

He turned then from the cold rail of the bridge and retraced his steps homewards. A few yards on he stopped. Before him, above his head, a long branch of the walnut tree lay frozen against the hard, livid sky. Twined in and out of it, as though they had been threaded with a stalactite upon the bough, were ten icicles shaped like letters of the alphabet.

The first icicle was shaped like a letter 'V'; the second, very clearly, a bold letter 'I'; the third, a perfect right angle, the letter 'L'; the fourth –

But it will be obvious to the reader. Frozen upon the branch above him, in bold Roman capitals, each one a foot in height, were the deadly letters of that deadly phrase

VILE OLD OWL

At first he only wondered. It was so beautiful. So icily true. He reached up to try to touch the letters, but they were out of reach. Taking a stick he considered breaking one of them; but he could not bring himself to do this any more than a painter could have brought himself to scrape off a little colour from a finished canvas.

Inside the house the luncheon gong sounded, deep and portentous in the aphonic silence of the gathering snow. Quintin did not move. He was enthralled. Had anybody ever done this before? What mattered Australia now? What mattered anything? He prayed for continuation of the cold spell; the thaw, the wasting away to water of his ice words, would be harder to endure than the death of even the most gargantuan snow-man.

After lunch, he told himself, he would bring Miss Bond out to see for herself. He had no desire to be cruel. But she, worshipping at the shrine of veracity, would surely not wish to miss so rare a demonstration of truth? Frozen there against the sky, the insult ceased to be personal. Nobody, not even Miss Bond, could honestly fail to see that.

Anticipating the joy he was going to have, he moved to the house. Then again he stopped, not many yards from the lobby door, looking at an espalier against the mellow bricks. There again, were the frozen words, the same size, the same Roman capitals. Quintin ran closer to the wall. He saw that the icicles were not joined to the espalier. They were simply standing out in the air, about a foot from the wall, supported by not so much as a spider's web. As before, they were beyond his reach.

He blinked and shook his head. His first pride gave way to uneasiness. The words on the tree had enchanted him; but these – they were too independent. He turned back in bewilderment to the walnut tree. Frozen on the same branch, Miss Bond's condemnation was still there. He looked again to the wall and sighed with relief. No words hung in the still air; he must have imagined them.

His mother appeared at the lobby door and called crossly.

'Quintin, come in. What are you standing about like that for?'

He ran up to her.

'I'm sorry, Mother, I'm awfully sorry. I just had to try my new skates.'

He wanted at once to drag her down to the walnut tree to show her what he had made. But there was no need. For there, forged in the air above him, though he did not at first see them directly, were the three fatal words; he knew they were there because of a sudden coldness over his head. He looked up. Yes, immediately above.

His mother frowned and took his arm.

'What are you looking at? What's the matter?'

'Can't you see, Mummy? Look!'

'There's nothing there, you funny boy.'

Irritated at being kept out in the cold, she dragged him inside and sent him to wash his hands and face.

A few minutes later Quintin came into the dining-room and took his place opposite Miss Bond. His father was away on business and for that he was glad. Nobody spoke. Mrs Claribel – who guessed from the governess's red eyes that there had been mutiny in the schoolroom – uncomfortably made some reference to the hard weather. When Simmons, the parlour-maid, had taken up the soup and for a moment left the room, Mrs Claribel said in an unhappy voice (for she disliked having to rebuke her only child), 'Quintin, come to see me in my work-room after luncheon.'

Quintin hardly heard the words. Terror clutched his young heart. For there, festooned above the luncheon table, some of the letters obscured in a bowl of early freesias, were the icy words which by now, he suddenly realized, he had come to dread.

He looked furtively at Miss Bond and his mother, then again at the words. It was obvious nobody could see them but him. The parlourmaid laid a plate before him; he was aware of her moving over to the corner table. But still, as though his very eyes were frozen, he stared at the words. His hands refused to grip the knife and fork. Hungry as he was he felt sick at the thought of the roast mutton on his plate. The clock ticked away; the silence grew unbearable.

'Eat your food, Quintin.' His mother, as she spoke, looked at him curiously. What was the matter with the boy, his eyes staring out of his head like that? Instinctively, she too looked in the direction he was following, a little above the freesias. There was nothing unusual about the flowers. What was wrong with the boy?

'Eat your food, Quintin.'

The words brought the truth forcibly before poor Quintin; he knew only too well what his food was. Miss Bond had told him. She knew. She knew everything.

He rose suddenly from his chair, reached out a trembling hand, snatched in the air and crunched the letter 'V' into his mouth. Shivering with the shock of so much ice on his tongue, he fell back again.

His mother cried out in a horrified voice –

'Quintin, are you ill?'

He did not answer. He still had nine letters to consume, nine bitingly cold letters. Oh, what a hateful thing the alphabet was! The prospect appalled him. But it would have to be done. Again rising, he snatched at the 'L' and bit half of it off, swallowing quickly. The warmth of his hand, still holding the other half of the letter, melted it. Drips of water fell upon the table. Mrs Claribel rose, her napkin held to her lips, and cried out –

'Simmons, come here – there's a lot of water – something must have gone wrong – '

Simmons ran up with a cloth. Meanwhile, Quintin had grabbed the 'L' and was cramming it whole into his mouth. All three women were standing, watching him in horrified fascination. Quintin was so completely preoccupied with his task, that nobody felt able to speak. A pool of water now lay on the table. With wet cold hands Quintin (now in a state of mystical exaltation) caught all that remained of the letters and dropped the chips of ice in a pile on to his bread plate.

'All right, Mother,' he said, 'don't worry. Everything's all right now.'

He felt very proud. He gave Miss Bond a sly smile hoping she would understand what he had been forced to do. But she, like the others, was completely bewildered.

'There must be – ' Mrs Claribel sat down slowly, ' – a crack in that waterjug. Simmons, take it away.'

She knew perfectly well that there was no crack; indeed the jug was still full of water. But she had forced herself to speak, so afraid was she of the possible truth – that her son had gone mad. Yet now his behaviour seemed normal. Unseen by her he had eaten all the ice on his plate; and now hungrily attacked his meat with the usual vigour of a healthy young boy. The meal passed in a strained silence. Immediately it was over, Quintin rushed outside to the walnut tree. His words were no longer there. He never saw them again. He had spoken; he had eaten; he was for the time being, cleansed.

He remembered that his mother had asked to see him after luncheon. So he went to her work-room ready for any rebuke. But she had nothing to say to him. Taking him in her arms she held him close and looked deep into his eyes. 'Dear boy,' she murmured. 'Dear boy.' She spoke as though she understood what had happened to him. But in truth, she did not. He was her only child and she was afraid for him.

★

From that day Quintin Claribel, once a lively child, became mysteriously silent; often even morose. His studies occupied much more of his time and Miss Bond had seldom cause to complain. His mother, who never forgot the extraordinary incident at the luncheon-table, watched him anxiously. The years passed and the cares of adult life, like a thunderstorm in May, seemed to be gathering round his head after too short a spring. And yet there was nothing actually wrong with him. Once or twice his mother asked, 'Is there anything on your mind, Quintin dear?' He was fifteen and she knew it was a difficult age. He read too much. There were books in the library which even her husband had never dragged to daylight, some of them – though reputed to be 'great' literature – not suitable for a boy of tender years. 'Is there anything on your mind, dear boy?' And he said, quite calmly, yes, there was a great deal on his mind. But he would not say more. So his mother, and even his sceptical father, began to imagine a great future for the curious being they had brought into the world.

Boyhood passed into youth and Quintin's tongue, particularly in winter, never once betrayed him. His elders remarked upon the purity of his language, his aptitude for precision, his search for the right word in a sentence and his extraordinary, though cold-hearted, courtesy. Nobody knew that, over and over again, in his bedroom on stark winter nights he had uttered unrepeatable words – words that could not have shocked his mother since she was ignorant of their meaning – hoping and yet dreading to see them frozen in the cold air. There was a night when he leaned out of the window, his hands and head numbed with coldness, and spoke softly and clearly into the dark icy air a stream of the vilest words a dictionary could offer. Trembling at his audacity, he waited silently. But the words had merely drifted into steam from his mouth. He shut the window and retired to bed, realizing finally that such deliberate and ponderous efforts could never yield a result. The obscene, the false, the unkind, the malicious – spoken dispassionately they meant nothing and were not destined to achieve the permanence of those three words spoken in bitterness so many years ago. The curse of his unique ability was simply this: it could never be *consciously* employed. He was destined to see, in ice, only those words which were the reflection of his deepest, unacknowledged thoughts. If he had ever again to eat ice, it would be the ice of the subconscious. Hence the fact that he was eternally on his guard, praised by his elders for his truthfulness and his almost pedantic speech – or, sometimes, for his discreet silences.

It was noticed that summer days brought to Quintin something of the common chatter and freeness of schoolboys. But with winter he was a changed being; on snowy days he barely spoke at all. Nobody knew how he suffered then; how much he wanted again to see the arctic fruits of his thoughts (who would not?) and yet how much he dreaded the consumption of them. He knew that 'Vile Old Owl' might only be a beginning. Suppose, one day, he were to utter some indiscretion from the sink of an unpurified mind, containing ten times as many words? One can easily imagine his predicament – longing for a repetition of the miracle, yet dreading it.

And so the youth became a young man, handsome, lithe and enigmatic. As the last months of school-days passed and various intellectual interests filled his mind, the curious incident of his childhood faded away into a half-forgotten dream, as unreal as the rocking horse in the attics. Miss Bond had long ago left Hassocks, the globes and exercise books were stowed away with other childish relics. The time came for Quintin to go to Oxford. There he was never very popular; although he soon earned distinction by reason of his impeccable manners. Whenever he entertained it was with an austere grandeur that impressed his guests. People said he was a 'deep one'. He came to learn the exclamations of silence, the power of the implied unspoken word, the deadlines of mere gesture. 'When Claribel shrugs his shoulders,' said somebody of him, 'you feel the world is balanced there, in a precarious state.' His few closer friends (the writer of this history was amongst them) seldom saw beyond the mask of his composure.

As would have been expected, he began to write; sombre,

balanced little essays, not sparkling but candle-lit by muted epigrams. He spoke at the Union and a diplomatic career was prophesied for him. But this was not his choice. When he came down he was determined to carve out (his own words) a unique place for himself in English letters. He would write, he said, perfectly. That was all. Perfectly. The value of the right word in the right place should be to him the *alpha* and the *omega* of his art. Only a very few people would appreciate him; but that did not matter. He was rich; he could afford to treat letters fastidiously; and it was the fastidious élite who would appreciate him.

His name was, at that time, coupled with that of the Honourable Ianthe Postle. She had a beautiful, if somewhat empty, face and Quintin, realizing that he was expected to make her his wife, felt that he might do worse. After all, she was the daughter of a Viscount. He was not in love, and he did not expect he ever would be. Words were his mistresses; and the studied phrase his bedfellow. Ianthe, apparently passionless as he was, would make a good partner. One aphorist at the breakfast-table was enough; and her misunderstanding of his most searing ironies would be a constant amusement for him.

All that summer and autumn the two young people were seen about together and on Quintin's twenty-first birthday, which was to be celebrated regally at Hassocks, everybody in the village of Anton and the surrounding country, hoped that an announcement would be made.

It was a party that lightened the gloom of an unusually cold November. All the estate tenants were invited to dinner; to them and the other guests Quintin made an exquisitely simple speech, polished to a wit only perceivable by the more intelligent. After the feast the several hundred guests put on coats and wraps and moved out to the terrace to watch the fireworks. There were long tables lit by crimson electric bulbs concealed amidst moss and ivy in the scooped-out boles of two oak trees; and on the tables, claret punch coffee, barrels of beer, cider, a puncheon of rum, cherry-brandy and many other warming drinks. Quintin, feeling suddenly a little embarrassed by this extravagant honouring of his manhood, slipped away to the orangery, hoping to be able to get a line right in his new ballade. To his extreme annoyance he found Ianthe in there. She was sad. To-night, she felt, it was time for Quintin to make her an offer; but he had showed no signs of doing so. He had, in fact, completely forgotten her existence.

She turned round, her face glowing in the light of the Chinese lanterns, and saw him coming in. For a moment he hesitated, wondering if he could get away. Then, realizing he might as well propose now as any other time, he made an opening, vague and yet in key.

'How exquisite this mimosa is.'

'Yes, it is jolly,' she said.

'How it makes one,' he continued slowly, 'long for the south – the south that ripens the vine and warms the blood.'

'Yes, the south is awfully nice.'

'There is something sad – ' he complained, ' – about these pyrotechnical arabesques.'

He drooped with a certain athletic grace into a basket chair, drawing his fingers across his forehead and smiling at Ianthe. It was a smile that always attracted people; a smile of singular humility, unexpected in one whose bearing was usually so arrogant. Actually, it was synthetic. He had worked hard to learn how to produce it at the right moment.

'Fireworks are like words,' he continued, (He was thinking, at what precise point shall I make my voice 'vibrate with passion?' Upon what word?) ' – like words, spoken – and too soon forgotten. But there are some words, Ianthe, which should be like a – '

'Oh look, Quintin!' she cried suddenly. 'Look at that heavenly rocket!'

His smile vanished. Without raising his head he looked at her malevolently under his heavy sensuous eyelids. What a noodle the girl was! Beautiful, no doubt; but it was mere pig-beauty. In a few years she would have lost all her charm. Still, a wife was useful; she kept other women away. Yes, he must propose; the tedious task must be accomplished as gracefully as possible.

Rising, he went near to her, preparing the right words, rolling them round and round silently on his tongue. Knowing that the moment had come, Ianthe waited, trembling a little, and closing her eyes. She felt his hand on her shoulder, very light; she heard him give a little cough. The next thing she heard was spoken with terrifying contempt – the single word,

'Noodle.'

She opened her eyes. 'W – what – did you say, Quintin?'

He bit his lip; he flushed.

'You called me a noodle!' she cried. 'I suppose I am not clever enough for you. How beastly of you, Quintin! After all these weeks when we have been so friendly. How cruel of you!'

'Wait – wait – ' he cried. And in a moment he was stammeringly excusing himself, as he had ten years ago in the schoolroom. 'I didn't mean it. I – I don't know what made me say it. I wasn't thinking of you, Ianthe darling. I swear I wasn't – '

He broke off. She had run out into the garden. He could see her, lit by the flaring light of a set-piece, disappearing towards the house, her handkerchief to her eyes. He started to pursue her; then stopped. What was the use of pretending he cared? He did not. He knew that he had, for the second time, reached a crisis in his life. Only one thing now had power to interest him. And that was –

He saw it in the distance, above the set piece. People were crying and clapping their hands and calling for him; his father ran towards him, dragging him along the terrace to see his birthday message burnt in words of fire against the sky. 'Many happy returns of the day.' He watched it and hardly saw it; watched the sizzling fiery words, man high, splutter away and shiver over like a falling house until there was nothing left but a few spitting embers and, high above, in monstrously large letters, spelt out in pure ice the deadly word 'NOODLE.'

He was, of course, enthralled – for a moment far too thrilled by this second demonstration of his power to think of the cold meal that lay before him. As before, nobody could see it but himself. Complaining of the sudden coldness people were moving back to the house; the tenants were struggling in to find their caps and coats. Quintin realized he was almost alone, except for one old man who, seeing that everybody had gone, was drinking the dregs from all the glasses remaining on the tables.

He ran suddenly, over to the place where the set piece had been burning. Glittering upon the black sky, so beautiful that his head reeled, was his new creation, NOODLE. Was it not, he thought, worth losing a thousand Ianthes to gaze upon such a thing?

Too high for him to reach, he stood there, gazing up at it, spellbound, hardly aware how cold he was until his name, called from the house, brought him to his senses.

Late that night when all had retired, he came down from his bedroom to a cupboard in the lobby where tools were kept. He returned with a small hammer. He had been unable to break the letters with his hands, the ice was so thick, the letters far too large to put whole into his mouth. Turning on the electric stove he contemplated his fate with a groan. It was intolerable that he should have to destroy this peerless work; intolerable, too, that he should have to digest so cold a meal – if it could be called a meal. And yet it was impossible to sleep with this chain of frozen letters which had re-appeared across the room. He knew, with a sickening certainty, that he would never get rid of them unless he ate them; and much as he admired the whole effect (particularly beautiful when the light was turned out) he knew that the constant presence of this word above him wherever he went, would have an undermining effect upon him. Better, obviously to eat it here, in the secrecy of his own room, than perhaps to betray himself in public as he had inno-cently done on the last and only other occasion. Tomorrow he had promised to address the local literary guild on the Sonnet. What if, in the middle of his discourse, so carefully written and rehearsed, this should appear – as very well it might?

Switching off the light, he left only the red glow of the stove so that he might at least have the aesthetic pleasure of seeing his work for the last time to the best advantage. Climbing up on a chair he seized one of the letters, the N, and was about to haul it down, when another idea came to him. He would be very cold. A plentiful supply of hot coffee would help a great deal. He had the night before him. Why not?

He left the room. In about a quarter of an hour, after a muddling search in the pantries and kitchen, he came back again with a saucepanful of boiling coffee and half a bottle of Cognac. Taking the hammer he again attacked the N. Laying it down on the carpet before the fire, he waited a while hoping it might melt. But no. He would have to go through with it. A pity, he mused, that this could not happen in summer. Perhaps it yet might. For one could have enjoyed even a dictionary on a hot summer's night.

For about ten minutes he continued his cold repast, thankful to find that at last the other letters were beginning to thaw; though, this perhaps was a doubtful blessing since they thawed over his bed, making it impossible for him to use it.

Finally he turned to the coffee and drank that. He did not, after all, touch the brandy. He was too depressed. Sitting there with his knees hunched up to his chin, by the fire, he contemplated the future. He did not complain; he accepted his fate; he bore Miss Bond no malice. He only wondered how best he could control and utilise this accomplishment through the long years of his life. He had never taken anyone into his confidence – except one friend (who is responsible for this history) and even that trusted friend had, he knew, been less sympathetic than amused. The secret must live and die with him; once it became common knowledge he could never be anything but ridiculous. Quintin Claribel, man-of-letters, would cease to exist; in its place the world would find a freak. Turning to his diary he wrote an account of the night's happenings. One day, perhaps, some use could be made of the theme. Not now.

So thinking, he dragged the mattress from the bed, threw aside the wet blankets, wrapped himself in rugs and dressing-gowns, and fell asleep before the fire.

At nine he was roused by Simmons who, seeing the wet bed-clothes, the recumbent form on the floor, the bottle of brandy by his side, rejoiced exceedingly to think that the young master was starting to sow his oats, and ran quickly down to the servants' hall to report the matter to cook, whose comments upon such excesses were known to be pungent and to the point.

The rest of that winter Quintin spent very quietly. He was, he said, writing a book, an occupation respected by his mother but not by his father, who could not see why the task should keep a young man so locked away from society. Quintin took but little interest in the affairs of the estate; the tenants, who had praised him on his twenty-first birthday party, now shook their heads critically. He was not like his father, they said. He didn't shoot, rarely rode, never talked to them over their garden gates. And what was the story about him and Miss Postle, whom he had bitterly insulted so that never again did she visit Hassocks?

One afternoon, late in March, Mr Claribel went up to his son's study, determined to have a frank talk with him. Had he spent so much on the education of his son for this to be his reward?

Quintin was writing and looked up irritably.

'I wanted to have a talk with you, Quintin,' began Mr Claribel.

'Yes, Father?'

'I don't understand what has come over you these last few months. Ever since your birthday you have been behaving very strangely. Is anything worrying you?'

'I am writing a book, Father. It occupies all my thoughts. I am sorry to seem so distrait.'

'A book *cannot* occupy all a man's thoughts. One would think you had no affection left for your parents.'

Quintin who had been in the middle of a particularly difficult sentence, said earnestly (hoping thus to get rid of his parent), 'I love and respect you, Father, above any man in the world. As for Mother, she is an angel.'

This was so feelingly said, the smile that accompanied it so charming, that Mr Claribel rose at once, convinced they had been misjudging the young man; he even accused himself of not taking enough interest in the book. It was obvious that it meant a great deal to him; and Mr Claribel, though he did not understand the high mysteries of art, always admired industry, whether of brain or body.

'Well,' he said, 'just try to be more sociable, my dear boy. That's all we ask. Come and play a game of billiards with me this evening. I rarely have anyone to play with and I'm sure some such relaxation would do you good.'

'I love billiards,' said Quintin absently. Already his fingers had reached for the pen. His father sighed and left the room; Quintin sighed too, with relief, and went on writing.

Just before tea he took a turn in the park. He had not been out all day. The wind was blowing from the east; there would perhaps be frost that night; possibly even snow. Quintin, in spite of this, felt very happy. His book was going well and he was confident that he now had his tongue under complete control. Nevertheless, it would be pleasant when summer came and he could relax a little.

It was the sort of day when the first wheatears arrived and he walked on to a high field, where on other days of early spring, he had seen the grey and white birds and been thrilled by the prophecy of summer that they brought. In the middle of the field, high up, with Hassocks House, a solid eighteenth-century building far away beyond the knoll of scots pines – he stopped. There were no birds. But there was something else that filled him with apprehension and drove all thoughts of summer out of his mind. Faintly, in the darkening sky, he could see, not many yards beyond him, some words. They did not make up a complete sentence. All he could read was: '... and respect you ... ab ... any man in ... Mother is an ang....'

He stared, thunderstruck. He shivered and rubbed his icy hands together, cramped by a day with the pen. He could not even place the sentence that the words vaguely suggested; he could not fill in any of the gaps. 'Mother is an ang ...?'

He racked his brain to remember; but he could not remember having said anything about Mother. All day, surely, he had been busy on his book; his father had tiresomely interrupted him, and he had said something merely to get rid of him. What?

It was obvious that the broken words he saw were hardly frozen yet, the thermometer had not dropped enough. Perhaps by morning the temperature would rise and he would be safe. But it was very disquieting nevertheless. He hurried home, upstairs to his room, and sat down. He felt very weakened by what he had seen. He had said nothing unkind all day; his thoughts had been exclusively concerned with his work. What could it mean?

At tea-time, anxious to restore himself to his father's confidence, he nodded his head quite eagerly when it was suggested that tomorrow he might try out a new pony.

'Unless the weather is too hard,' said his father, helping himself to cake and thinking happily that their son was, after all, a very good son.

Quintin made no comment. Like the child of twelve years ago he sat staring in front of him. Blazing in their full icy glory, encircled like a coronet above Mr Claribel's bald head, were the words 'I love and respect you, Father, above any man in the world. As for Mother, she is an angel.' They were smaller than previous words; each letter no more than an inch in height. But they were shockingly clear; shockingly attractive. Of all his works this, undoubtedly, was the most finished, the most graceful. It had none of the ingenuousness of 'Vile Old Owl'; none of the vigorous brutality of 'Noodle'. This was the fastidious product of a more adult genius.

Without a word he rose and left the room. He was very shocked. Surely, what he had said had been true? He did love his father; his mother was an angel. No! It was not true. He did *not* love his father; his mother might very well be an angel, but what cared he? He had spoken only in order to get rid of a parent who, in fact, he regarded as a tiresome old bore without a single original thought beneath his hairless scalp. Dismayed by this realization, Quintin nearly wept. He was brought very low.

The words were circled round the electric light shade. He could not bring himself to eat them yet; he could not feel that he had been justly treated. But it was clear, it was clear from the way they hovered over his finger bowl during dessert, that they demanded to be eaten.

'You are shivering, Quintin,' remarked his angelic mother. 'Are you cold?'

'No. No,' he muttered, looking away from her, not caring to meet her gentle eyes. He heard his father saying, 'Shall we play billiards, Quintin?'

He rose abruptly. 'Yes.' Anything for action. Preceding his father to the billiard room he found his cue and whipped the cover from the table. Soon, they were silently immersed in the game and for perhaps twenty minutes, all went well. Quintin played indifferently but with style; his father played brilliantly. The shameful circlet had not reappeared since dinner and Quintin began to hope that, after all, fate had played him an unjust trick and had now repented. Outside the snow was falling. He was aware of the horrible dangers that surrounded him and he longed to be completely alone.

'You are very quiet,' said Mr Claribel. He smiled and nodded pleasantly, not daring to allow himself a word. His father was crouching low over the table, intent upon a break. As he was about to aim his cue at the red, he was jerked in the back by Quintin who had leaned forward, under the shaded green light, and was clutching wildly at something in the air.

'What in God's name are you doing?' cried Mr Claribel. 'Can't you see I'm in the middle of a shot?'

'I can't help that,' mumbled Quintin whose mouth and hands, to his father's amazement, were dripping wet.

'Are you going to have a fit or something?' snapped Mr Claribel. But Quintin again made a snatch at the air and brought his hand to his open mouth. In doing so he dropped a piece of ice on the table – it was, as a matter of fact, a hemisphere of the letter B. At the sight of the water on the table, Mr Claribel went wild.

'Where the devil is all this water coming from?' he shouted. 'Burst pipe – burst pipe – ' and he ran to the door calling for everybody whose name he could remember.

While he was gone, presumably in search of an amateur plumber, Quintin hastily consumed the rest of the sentence – 'I love billiards' – which had suddenly shot out of the void above him, just as his father was about to take his shot. It had been too much for him. Such chilly mockery, so glacial an echo of words reminding him all too coldly that, indeed, he loathed the game of billiards – this had been too much for him. He was, for the first time, almost glad to eat his words. And having eaten them he hurried away from the room, unable to face his father's wrath when he should see the puddle on the table.

Locking his door he sank on his bed. Nobody came to him until, much later, his mother knocked; he begged her to leave him, and she reluctantly did so. All night he lay on his bed with his clothes on. He felt doomed; he could face no more English winters. The life of a Trappist, vowed to perpetual silence, was perhaps the only future in store for him.

Towards dawn he ate *'I love and respect you father above any man in the world as for mother she is an angel'*. All these hours it had been waiting around a silver tankard on the dressing-table. He gulped it down in one great gulp, before any of it had time to thaw. It was, he presently wrote in his journal, the one utterance of his which he consumed entire.

After that, life was never the same with his parents. Summer passed quite happily, but winter, he knew, could not be postponed. In October he announced his intention of travelling south. He was never again to return to England.

He found the south of France greatly to his liking. There was rarely any frost and on those occasions when cold weather did come, he stayed quietly in his villa and saw nobody. He was waited upon by a deaf and dumb servant, called Jocelyn, who had been the blacksmith's son in the village at home, a youth who had never received much kindness and was full of gratitude to his young master. They must have been a strange couple. It is said that they were more like friends than master and servant, and would often be seen setting off for the day in the car, in pursuit of rare birds, a study that engaged much of the time not given to writing. There were, certainly, occasions when Quintin had to eat his ice but Jocelyn seems to be ignorant of the circumstances and nothing definite is known. Indeed, those years are remarkable for their obscurity; Quintin seems to have had no close friends at all and, from what can be gathered, his life was remarkably discreet and pure.

Meanwhile, his first, his second and his third books were published. They were exquisitely written and evoked praise from the exquisite quarters. His parents, who had sorrowfully abandoned him to his own devices, wrote kindly of these successes and suggested a visit to Hassocks. 'The house is so dull without you. We never have any parties, nobody comes to see us.' But their letter had the misfortune to arrive in midwinter, and Quintin, though he wrote back quite affectionately, was not to be enticed away.

It was not, in fact, until his thirtieth year that any move was made. In that year, having just finished his fifth book, he accepted the offer of a furnished house in Switzerland which some friends had unexpectedly to leave. He knew perfectly well the dangers that lay ahead in a country where snow and ice are as common as grass in England. And he went there deliberately; for two reasons. 'I am now,' he wrote, 'surely old enough to have complete control of my speech.' (And, indeed, those who met him declared it was remarkable that a man who wrote such impeccable English should have so little to say.)

His second reason; he was actually tempted to make experiments in a country colder than any he had so far visited. He felt that the time had come for him to face up to this accomplishment of his, for so long kept secret from the world. Intending to write a book upon the matter, it was desirable, even necessary, that he should test the power of his tongue to the uttermost. He never expected that he would be able deliberately to create glacial words; he had, alas! tried that too often – spending, sometimes, weary hours on bitter nights speaking his own poems aloud into the still frozen air, with no result whatever except a sore throat. But he decided that he would simply withdraw the guard he had placed upon his speech; he would even loosen his tongue with drink, mix freely with the types of people he detested, and observe the results. Was there not something attractive, too, in the idea of Quintin Claribel, the brilliant essayist, the remote man of letters, never seen by the press, never once interviewed – suddenly completely changing the manner of his life?

So he went to Switzerland, having first taken the precaution of ordering three large refrigerators to place in the house. They might possibly come in useful. He had already, on one awful occasion, had to consume an ode, full of classical references, written by a dead friend of his which he had quoted before a select company as his own work; it had been an immense and unpleasant meal and he did not want a repetition of it. The refrigerators would, perhaps, serve as storing places for future phenomena; a line, a word, even a comma, could be taken a day as he felt inclined.

Packing off his fifth manuscript to the publisher, Quintin set off with Jocelyn, joyfully looking forward to a new sort of life. He had, for too long, led a monastic life – and all because he was afraid of a few meals of ice. It was ridiculous. There should be a change to all this. Were he to die in the attempt, he would, at any rate, leave an amazing book behind him.

He did die in the attempt and he did not leave an amazing book behind him. It was all very sad and totally unexpected. On his first night in Switzerland, he came down from his mountain home, intending to spend the evening at the inn where, he was told, a number of English tourists had arrived. He felt in need of company, particularly the company of English people. In this mood, ready for adventure, he entered the inn and joined the rowdy throng of young people, many with skis and snow-boots, back from a day's sport.

To his delight a party of young men and women, seated

round a large table drinking beer, was discussing literature. For some moments he hovered near them, listening. They were talking of style, and one of them brought up the name of George Moore. 'Surely,' said the earnest speaker, 'the greatest stylist in the English language?'

Quintin said, slowly and quietly, 'Can one think of Moore as anything but a laboured pedant? Pedestrian art, surely?'

The remark, of course, made an impression. It was unusual in those days to criticize Moore and the stranger bore the mark of authority in his quiet pleasant voice. One of the young men, his name was Powell, invited him to sit with the company. Quintin willingly did so, calling for drinks for all with a graceful lack of ostentation. It was not long before he was discoursing at some length upon writers and writing. He talked with a sombre distinction, quoting smoothly from writers as far apart as Spenser and Rudyard Kipling. He made no attempt to guard his speech. It would have been obvious to any listener that, in him, a rare Parliamentarian had been lost to England. There was nothing in what he said which could have been interpreted as malicious, pompous or untrue. Certainly nothing indecorous. Quintin, since those unhealthy experiments of his youth, had always been pure of speech. He never even swore. His talking was remarkable for its almost unperceivable ironies.

After the discussion had been going on for about an hour, there was a slight pause. Quintin sipped his beer happily, wondering why he had denied himself such pleasures as this for so long. Then Powell – wishing, as youth always does, to wind up the argument to some definite conclusion – said to him, 'Who would you say, Sir, is the greatest living master of English prose?'

Everybody waited on his answer. They did not, of course, know the identity of the charming stranger, and Quintin enjoyed their company all the more because of this. He was really a very modest man. As he revolved the answer to Powell's question in his mind, a score of famous names passed under consideration. It was, therefore, with a truly terrible shock that, a moment afterwards, he heard himself saying, calmly and authoritatively –

'Quintin Claribel.'

From a few there was a murmur of doubtful agreement; others uncertainly shook their heads; one said, quite flatly, 'Never heard of him'. Miserably, Quintin sought for some means to withdraw his statement. He knew at once that he had fallen very low. There were several writers, he knew, who wrote better than he could; wrote more firmly, more squarely, less fussily. An honest critic, he actually placed himself by no means at the top of the list. And yet he had declared that Quintin Claribel was the greatest living master. What did it mean? Could it mean that in the depths of his mind he believed it to be true?

He began to stammer a few words. 'No – no – I – I didn't mean that. Quintin Claribel is not – I mean – '

Suddenly he turned and left them abruptly, to their surprise and disappointment. An old gloom returned. He felt afraid, very friendless.

Slowly he returned to his villa. So far nothing had happened. Perhaps, after all, his immediate penitence had saved him; or perhaps (he brightened exceedingly) Quintin Claribel *was* the greatest living master of English prose? In the still cold night he almost ran up the steep path, so anxious was he to refer to his four published works and deliver judgement upon himself.

Jocelyn was waiting up for him and looked at him, as he came in, with a smile that meant 'Do you want me for anything?' Almost roughly Quintin pushed him aside, went straight to the bookshelves, and found his own austerely bound works. Piling cones on the fire he fell down on some cushions and started to read. It was very quiet, so quiet that he strained his ears expecting some sound which never came. He went on reading, page after page, essay after essay. Finishing one book he started sleepily to read the second as the clock struck two. The fire had almost died and he realized how intensely cold

he was. He could read no more; and he did not want to. The
work was mediocre; he knew, he had known from almost the
first page, that it was mediocre. Wearily he reached for the
most recent collection; opened a page at random and read. It
was still mediocre; it was merely a more finished mediocrity.
What he had said, he had certainly always said well; but the
purity of the style could not hide the paucity of the matter.
If these works had been by any other writer, he would have
thrown them on the fire. Thrown them on the fire? Well, why
not? It was the only honest gesture to make.

Wearily, yet with a fine sense of the rightness of his action,
he threw all four books on to the dying fire, struggled to his
feet and mounted the stairs to his bedroom. Cynically he
reviewed his life; what had it been but a mere waste of words?
He realized now that words had enslaved him from the beginning. Even at the font, he must have sensed the loveliness of
his own Christian name. He remembered how his parents had
told him of his extraordinarily intelligent and attentive behaviour at his Baptism, as though he understood the mystery that
was being enacted in him. But, the truth was, even then, a babe
in long clothes, he had been entranced merely by the glorious
music of his own name.

'Quintin Claribel,' he murmured, on his way up the
stairs, 'Quintin Claribel.' Better, far better, than magic casements; indeed, these two words, he now saw, had always been
for him the magic casements which opened to the perilous
sea of words. He had called himself a man of letters. Of *letters*. Yes. Even the appearance of each letter thrilled him and
always had. He remembered that 'O' on the ice when he had
skated twenty years ago; he remembered his first creation on
the bough of the walnut tree; the beauty of all his frozen crea-
tures through the years. And, with all this in mind, he pushed
open the bedroom door.

It would not quite open; something stood in the way. Irritably – pleased now with his train of recollection and resenting
any disturbance of it – he forced the door forward. It burst
open with a strange tinkling crash; he found himself sprawling

against the lintel to save himself from falling. He was standing, though he did not at once realize it, before his *magnum opus*.

He switched on the light.

'Good God!' he said.

He ought to have known it; he ought to have expected it. Larger than any letters he had ever seen, each one three feet in height, stretching right the way across the room from window to window like a great hurdle, he faced his own name in solid ice.

'QUINTIN CLARIBEL'

One letter, the 'N,' which had been near the door, had been broken by his carelessness and lay in shattered pieces at the end of the word. So what he read was 'Quinti Claribel'. Quinti – Quinti! He rocked and roared with wild, ironic laughter. How absurd it immediately became! Why had nobody, in his child-hood, given him that nickname, saving him perhaps, from the enslavement of words? Had he been called 'Quintie' (and even in his present mood he could see the added ridiculousness an 'e' on the end would give to it), he might have been a different person.

Carefully he climbed through the space left by the 'N' and surveyed the whole work from the other side. He liked it just as well backwards. From all angles it was a perfect creation – even though disfigured. It would, he saw, take a very long time to eat.

For an hour he sat there, looking at his creation. He knew that this was the final crisis; if he could bring himself to devour all this ice, he might be different, perhaps a better person. But could he do it? Could he swallow, piece by piece, the pigmy-high letters of his own dulcet name?

Towards dawn, knowing that he must make the attempt, he wrote some notes in his journal. Then he stretched his half-frozen limbs, put some gloves on his stiffened hands and reach-ing out for a chunk of the 'N' which still lay in several pieces on the floor; brought it to his mouth and bit a little piece. He swallowed; he bit more; he swallowed again. He began to feel within himself a curiously shrinking sensation; not altogether unpleasant but certainly very watery. He took another piece of the 'N' with uncertain fingers and swallowed that too with a great gulp. For a moment he paused. Then a wild passion seized him, like the first incoherent passion of a young boy in love. With both hands he furiously attacked the ice, breaking it down and pouncing with eager, open mouth upon any piece nearest to him. All the precision which had marked every action of his life, left him. Almost immediately the thaw began. A delicious sensation flooded his vitals. Not only was the ice thawing; he himself was thawing.

The dawn broke over the mountains and a ray of steely sunlight glanced through the half-drawn curtains. Jocelyn, sleeping in a room below Quintin's, noticed a patch of dampness on the ceiling and wondered vaguely what it was. He turned over and went to sleep. Half an hour later he was awakened by a dripping of water upon his upturned face. He rose, puzzled; dressed, and went to the kitchen to make his master some tea. Going upstairs, he knocked on the door and went in.

He was so shocked by what he saw that the cup of tea crashed from the tray to the floor. The bed was empty and had never been slept in. His master's clothes, soaking wet, were lying in a heap in the middle of the room. Floods of water had soaked through the carpet to the boards, through the boards to his own room below. It was bitterly cold.

From that day to this Quintin Claribel has never been seen. It was assumed that he must have gone up to the mountains early that morning in search of a Snow-breasted Eagle, a rare bird that he had mentioned in conversation at the Inn the night before. But we, who have access to his diaries, know better.

VII

In the Steam Room

In the steam room the physical body is wrung out of you, and yet you become most painfully aware of it. As you open the door to the dank lobby which leads to the inner door and pause there a moment before approaching this forbidden threshold, you are aware of a sense of the ridiculous, standing there naked, already drenched in your own sweat, your skin flabby and salmon pink, yet asking for more. You wonder what made you pay your money for the ambiguous luxury of a Turkish Bath. You almost turn back from that second door. It is not exactly inviting; and the earlier part of the ceremonial debilitation of your winter-weakened body has been more of an undermining of your whole nervous system than anything else, only serving to emphasise the naked fact that this body which you so cherish is doomed to extinction, whatever manner of ending is to embrace it. No: it is not altogether a pleasant experience, wandering with a neutral linen cloth round your middle (or discarding it if you so wish) from room to room where other unclothed men, mostly middle-aged, sprawl inertly in steel deck chairs, lie out on benches, pad about like neurotic leopards on the hot stone floor, or go to the showers to wash away the grey sweat which has been sucked out of their pores. Not altogether pleasant, but oddly fascinating; and it is this fascination, this unholy masochism which finally drives you towards the second door, and the steam room.

Such thoughts passed in my mind as I faced that door. I was really rather weary of this body of mine by now. Outside, a superb morning of early spring was blooming; one ought to be walking high in the hills or lying in the sun, not stuck in a

clammy town and going through this almost obscene performance of trying to restore a body which was well past its prime.
About ready for the knacker's yard, that's what I am, I told
myself. And then I pushed open the heavy door and entered
the steam room. I was, so to speak, in the condemned cell.

Ferocious whirling clouds of saturating steam made it
impossible at first to see anything at all. For a few moments it
seemed unbearable and I nearly gave it up. The steam coiled
and eddied, lapping at the substance of the solid square room
and at once snaking at me as though to macerate me deep in
its own essence. The door closed behind me, and I was alone
– or thought that I was alone. Because at first I did not see the
one other inmate; and even when I did begin to see him lying
belly down on the slatted bench along by one wall, I was still
alone. In the steam room, even when there are others present, you are always strangely alone. It is quite impossible to
imagine holding a conversation with anyone in there. Even
Socrates would have dried up. The silence is unbreakable and
any desire to break it is soon quelled by the very weight of the
heat which presses down on you and by the sinuous vapours
which churn your body and seem to choke out your entire
personality.

At first I stood near the door, wondering how I was able
to breathe at all. Every breath became more of an effort. I
bent forward, resting my hands on my knees, and opening
my mouth felt the moisture dripping down my body. Then
I touched the end of the bench nearest to me, and drew my
fingers sharply away. Surely, not even a glutton for punishment
could sit on this? The heat seemed intolerable, and yet, in fact,
it was tolerable; and after a moment or two I did sit, leaning
forward and staring into the vapourised mobility of the room.

It was then I saw, on the far side, a tattooed arm hanging
down from the bench, and gradually there came into misty
view the rest of the other man's body, a large clumsy body
with streaks of wet grey hair on its back. I looked at the other
benches, but all were empty; there was only this one occupant,
and myself. I was glad to feel his presence; I might have been

uneasier without him. I tried to lie on my back, but the heat was too much and I felt if I so much as touched the stone wall I would sizzle and shrink to a wet cinder. I half expected to see the electric chair rise up from a trap door in the centre of the room. I saw a block of what looked like iron scooped out to make a neck rest, and similar blocks on the other benches. But I did not dare to touch it, feeling it would be red hot. I began to expect the skin to peel off my body layer by layer, until a raw piece of sinewy meat would be all that was left of me. And then I wondered how much of this it was wise to take; whether a point would be reached when it would be impossible for me to make the supreme effort to reach the door and get out.

Sense of time began to waver; had I been in here one minute, two, or even ten? And what was the longest span of time one could endure with safety? An odd pride began to govern the me who seemed to have become a distillation of the body I had brought in, and was now floating around in this gyration of steam – a pride which told me I must not weaken till the other man had gone. But he had not moved so far as I could judge; he was still in the same position. By now I could see the pink soles of his feet, the fat and flattened thighs, the wrinkled buttocks, the hairy back, and the neck crouched in upon the block. How could he bear it? For how long had he been roasting? Probably he was well accustomed to the tyrannies of the Turkish Bath and knew just how much of the steam room he could take, unlike myself who had only used it once before in my life, and then not here. An ardent balneologist, perhaps, given to boasting of his experience. No. I was not going to be beaten by this man; what he could suffer I could suffer. And so, gingerly, with a great deal of trepidation, I offered my back to the wood slats, stretched out my legs, and closed my eyes.

I began then to think of death. At the age of fifty-six you do think of death rather more often than you wish, and it can become disquieting. How would the end come? Always assuming it was an end ... Peacefully, with those I loved and who loved me, at my bedside. Absolution given, the Host on my tongue, the prayers for the dying distant in my ears? After a stroke, with limbs paralysed, speech distorted, vision impaired? Aided by merciful drugs to lose the pain of a cancer? Alone, struggling to find the way home in a snow drift? Dragged down by the crash of a wave, or hurled broken on a spine of rock? The operative figure in a bedraggled and shameful procession to the gallows? Crushed to a raw bleeding mess by a nose to nose meeting of car and lorry? Falling from the triforium of a cathedral and knowing, in the air, that the flagstones were bound to be splashed and spattered by blood and brains? On the operating table, intestines laid indecently bare, the surgeon cutting through to an enlarged appendix? Drifting to a fog of remorse after supper of barbiturate and whisky? The roof of the mouth blown to bits by my own gun? Licked by tongues of fire in a top storey hotel room? Dragging the unwanted old body to some rank dustbin with mildewed bread crushed down on top of a mush of tea-leaves soggy in newspaper? By axe, knife, or guile of poisoner? Fallen forward on the lavatory seat in one last defeated effort to evacuate bowels? By interior haemorrhage, the crash of a fist, or broken bottle splintered in the eyes? Slowly, unknowingly, face upwards in a hot bath? Or face downwards in....

There were as many ways of dying as there were of living, and, for all I knew, one of those ways might now have come to me unless I could urge my palpitating body up from this blistering bench towards the door. There were ways of dying which perhaps had never yet been imagined, unimaginable as once had been the searing pains which ate into Hiroshima, and slower than the unfolding of the glory of spring. Slow, too slow; and again – quick, too quick – as when the hands of a murderer both lost and took control, and smothered you head downwards on a wooden bench in the steam room of a Turkish Bath; then, having attacked unseen, left you to rot away in the heat with the door locked, left your carcase to be found hours later and taken from hence to the cold slab of the mortuary, there to suffer the final humiliation of identification.

I forced my stupefied nine stone up from the bench, hid-
eously fascinated by these images (of the ways of dying). It was
dreadfully true that I could not with certainty declare that my
way out would not be one of these ways. But one way I would
not go; not in the steam room, the breath pumped out of me,
the lungs bursting. It was possible to avoid that.

Yet, suppose the door would not open? Suppose it had been
locked on the other side because of some fault in the mecha-
nism of the heating – and why not? For no one had seen me
enter so far as I knew. I remembered that there were few others
in the Baths that morning. And now the silence, smothered
by the confluence of steam, burst and gurgled in my ears, my
throat was rough as sandpaper, my eyes streaked with sweat
that seemed the colour of blood. I dragged myself up, sat, and
looked down at my legs. They seemed to taper away to slimy
strands of seaweed in a dank cave. With all that foetid heat I
yet felt cold. I *was* cold; and I was trembling. And I crouched
forward as though to begin a race – a race I must make to the
door.

I don't exaggerate these fancies; and I don't exaggerate the
horrible relish with which I indulged such images and then,
with a pent-up sigh of relief, turned to look to the other
bench, determined to make some remark, merely in order to
have the consolation of a response from my companion. It was
an absurd comfort to know he was there, probably dreaming of
past pleasures, of lovers who had shared their younger bodies
with his, of luxurious meals and rare wines; perhaps, even now,
ageing as he was, contemplating richer pastures. If the door
was locked, had been locked in error, with his company this
could be lightly met. We would both shout, and bang, and bang
again, till one of the attendants would come, full of apologies;
and I would be able to tell the story of how I was nearly stifled
to my end in the steam room and was only saved by a sense of
humour which I and the other man found we both shared.
Perhaps I would come to know him well, we might even
become close friends, and in extreme old age take a delight in
recalling the oddity of our first encounter with one another.

I think I tried humour. I think I said, 'Why don't you turn over and roast the other side' (thinking of the Roman Martyr Lawrence, on the grid-iron). But whatever I said, no answer came. I looked across to the arm hanging down, with the finger tips nearly to the floor. And then I seemed to see something else: a thin red trickle coming slowly from the slats by his head. And there was a smell in the place, a smell of sickly corruption.

I moved a little closer, then suddenly stopped. I realised there were no feet displayed on the bench; no spreadeagled thighs, no buttocks, back, neck, or head. . . .

I was alone in the steam room. The door had not opened since I came in. I had been alone all the time.

Of course the door was not locked, and of course I got out, panting, weakened by the sweat which blinded me, and moving on legs which seemed to have shrivelled to sticks. Falling into one of the deck chairs in the adjoining chamber I tried to admit a sense of relief into me. But it would not come. My heart thumped and stuttered, and I began to want to return to the steam room to certify what I had not seen; what, it appeared, I must have imagined. But too vividly I remembered the coiling scarlet streak of colour on the floor of the colourless, engulfing room (like a painting by Francis Bacon); something which had been dribbling from the head of the man I had seen, or thought I had seen, lying face down on the bench. Very good, then: so there had been blood. I had imagined that too. Macabre inventions fester in the mind easily when the body is weakened; and I had come to the Baths in a weak condition, tired and burdened by worries. I had hoped to lose them here. But it had been a mistake – one that I warn others never to make.

But *had* there been another man there? And had I merely never heard him leave as I lay, muted and steamed, on the slats? Or had my desire for company embodied him in my imagination? Either was possible; and now I began to watch the outer door to the steam room, hoping that the other inmate would emerge, if there had been another – and I hoped so; it would be more comfortable if this were so.

Nobody came out. Perhaps three minutes passed. A thin lank man, almost altogether hairless, passed me and went towards the shampoo room; and a short paunchy man with a Jewish face fell into the chair next to mine with a grunt of satisfaction. Both were in their fifties. It was impossible to place them, except that by their lack of muscle it was clear they did not do heavy manual labour. One might have been a bishop, the other an accountant. It didn't matter; they were only flesh and blood here, and male. I looked at the key of my cubicle, attached to my wrist by its strap, and thought with deliberate pleasure of the soothing rest I would soon have on the cubicle bed, after massage in the shampoo room, the final shower, the cold refreshing dip and the rough invigoration of the outsize bath towel I would take from the attendant's office. But this pleasurable thought was beaten down by renewed apprehension. I could not relax until I had been again to the steam room to find out if there was another man there, or not. And I began to dread that second visit. What would I really find?

There was movement in front of me. I looked up. Somebody was going to the steam room. I did not see his face as he disappeared into the lobby; but he was a tall cumbersome man and I had seen his back. It was covered with hair. And his arms were tattooed.

Now it is a fact about the male of the species that he grows hair almost anywhere, but not so commonly on his back, between the shoulder blades. I was certain that this man was the one I had seen, or thought I had seen, in there a few moments ago. Was he so soon going in for a further steaming? I wanted to make some remark to the man next to me; but he was snoring, and it is not good etiquette to address a stranger in the Turkish Bath. The word 'Silence' is displayed everywhere, and it is generally respected. So I waited, tensed now, disliking every second. I longed to leave the place and get out into the March sun; the experience had become tainted. But there was something I had to see through. I waited.

In another half minute a second man passed me and also went towards the lobby. I would have recognized him without the scarlet slip he wore on his nakedness; he was one of the attendants, who had taken my ticket and shown me to cubicle number seven: a man of powerful build, with a waxy military moustache, hectic colouring on his cheekbones, a curiously theatrical figure. Ex-RSM, perhaps. And he had seemed to me in some way like a Turk — the genius of the Bath — its famil-iar. A pantomime being, with something of clockwork in his movements; and in his fixed unnatural smile too much show of very white teeth. One of those men who overdo the body business. His chest was tattooed. And his body was taut with muscle, his hands very large and white, yet with red protuber-ant knuckles.

He opened the door labelled 'steam room' and passed out of view. I closed my eyes, trying to become detached from action which, I told myself, had nothing to do with me. But all the time I was invaded by fears I could not rightly interpret. I tried to pull myself out of the chair to go to the steam room again. But it could not be done. I stayed, eyes closed, seeing again that scarlet rivulet on the stone floor.

Again I was aware of movement. The paunchy man next to me was reading a newspaper, his left hand picking at the soft-ened skin on his left heel. I saw the attendant coming out from the steam room. He walked quickly and silently past me.

I got up suddenly. The whole thing had now become absurd; why should I feel this involvement? Why accept it? Sti-fling questions, blacking out images, I went back to the show-ers I had already used when I first came in. I washed myself down from head to foot with soap, feeling like Pontius Pilate after he had given Barabbas to the crowd. Then I went quickly towards the shampoo room. The quicker I got out of this place the better, I said. But I had to have my money's worth; and I greatly looked forward to the massaging of my flac-cid body. Perhaps it would erase the discomfiture which had fallen, unbidden, upon me.

I lay on my back on the stone slab in the shampoo room and rested my head on the scooped-out head-rest. I closed my eyes. This was the essential pleasure of the Turkish Bath and I gave myself to it unreservedly. Outwardly as cleansed as by the first lavation after birth, I waited for the therapy of the masseur. He came almost immediately to me, and I did not open my eyes as he began to soap me, then work his pliable fingers along my tired and relaxed body. This was altogether an impersonal act, but I permitted myself the words 'marvellous weather'. He made no verbal response. But suddenly his fingers became tensed. For a moment he stopped. I smelt his breath, very close to me. It was slightly sour. I opened my eyes.

I was looking up to the moustached raw face of the attendant who had gone into the steam room. This was a shock, because I had not realised he was also one of the masseurs. But this was not, I knew, the only reason why his ministration came as a shock. While I saw his white teeth and felt his strong fingers working round my ribs I knew that presently he would ask me to turn over. I said something. I said, 'The heat in the steam room was almost more than I could take today.' (And I added 'today' as if to make it clear that I was a practised devotee of the rituals of the Turkish Bath.) To this, he made no comment. With a fixed expression, he only said, 'Turn over, will you please sir?'

I did. And as his hands began to knead down my back to my loins a sudden rising sickness glotted in my throat. I swallowed. 'Stop a second,' I said. 'I'm not comfortable.' He stopped. I moved my head a little. He asked, 'Ready now, sir?' I murmured yes, I was ready. And now his hands smoothed and slid over my thighs and buttocks, then to my shoulder blades, curving round the nape of my neck. The nausea seeped up in me again. I felt his thumbs. My face was pressed close down to the slab and I could not get into an easy position. I again asked him to stop. But now he took no notice; and as I tried to yield my body to his manipulation I felt a horrifying sense of urgency, in him and in myself. From him — an intuition that he was playing for time, that he had to keep me here; in myself, fear which became terror. For what did I know about this man, who now had mastery of my body? What did I know of his past? Of the earlier activities of those hands?

His hands were now pressing at the top of my spine. Then he thumped me lightly, several times. He was hurting me. I tried to assure myself this could not be helped; it would be ridiculous to complain. After all, the man was a professional; he knew precisely how to deal with the pains of middle-age. Perhaps too precisely ...

My head swam. Into my imagination lurched back the man in the steam room, the blood from the inert head. There was a harsh dryness in my nostrils and throat. Death could come quickly, yet never quickly enough under certain conditions. And death was not so much the enemy as was the manner in which it chose to come, seizing as its means a chance encounter with one whose dreadful deed had so nearly been witnessed. Did he know that I knew? And had there been other victims before the man who, dead or alive, might now be still in the steam room?

I heard someone speaking. 'Jake, I can't get into the steam room! Has something gone wrong with the door?'

The hands were lifted suddenly away. I gasped, and an intense relief filled me. I turned over, pulled myself up.

'I'm sorry, sir.' Jake spoke. Another man was standing beside him, the man who sat in the chair next to me just now. 'I had to lock it. Something wrong with the regulator – or ventilation blocked, maybe. I was just going to tell the other gents.'

'Damn' nuisance! Reckon we should have a rebate on this – don't you agree?' He had addressed me.

'I used the room,' I said. 'It was – certainly – very hot.'

The other man moved away. I forced myself to look at the attendant. 'Someone went in,' I said, 'just after me.'

'Yes, sir.' His eyes were an unreflecting blue, cold as stones; his words were on one level note. 'I found the gent and saw he wasn't comfortable. So I called him out, and locked up till I can put it right.'

He moved away from me. 'Kindly take a shower, sir,' he said, 'if you intend to use the cold bath.'

I took the shower, and washed away the pressure of his hands. Quickly I plunged my body into the cold pool in the adjoining room. But there was none of the relaxed exhilaration this should have given me. I went back to the long rest room, found a towel and dried myself. I looked at the half dozen or so men who reclined in the arm-chairs. None of them had tattoos on their arms ...

I heard Jake talking to a colleague. 'I'll slip down to the boiler room and see if I can fix it.' He was pulling on a sweater over his shirt. I saw him go out. A few moments later I left too, glad to find the sun and breathe even the fumes of the city.

Jake did not return, nor was the steam room used. When the door was unlocked an Italian, who had recently opened a restaurant in the city, was found dead, lying face downwards on a bench, his nose blocked with blood. He had been suffocated by pressure on his neck from behind, his face forced down to the slats.

Some days later the body of the attendant was dragged from the river. He had lived alone, a bachelor and ex-seaman, and although no motive for the crime was discovered it was openly surmised that he had been responsible, since it was found that there was no defect in the steam room. It was also found that he and the Italian had been at sea together twenty years earlier.

I shall never know whether I actually saw the body, dead or alive, in that place. I only know that the place smelt of death by violence, that the steam was fouled by coiling wreaths of the lust to kill, and that the hands of the killer pressed down upon my own body. The horror of the minutes I spent under the hands of the attendant never really leaves me.

And when I think, as I often do, of how my end might come, I tell myself I am certain of only one thing: it will not come, at the hands of a masseur, in the steam room of a Turkish Bath.

VIII

Flowers I Leave You

The piano, her husband's wedding present to her, was good company during most of the years of a frustrated marriage. Accompanying herself often alone, she would sing the popular songs of those Edwardian days. 'Down in the Forest,' 'Thoughts have Wings,' 'Where my Caravan has rested.' She was not a very competent pianist. E flat major was the key which best suited her florid style, and her fine, slender fingers were capable enough for the simple accompaniments of her songs which she would nearly always end with an arpeggio flourish. In defiant passion her rich contralto voice would ring out in the many suburban houses they rented in London during the hard years when post-war depression sent thousands on the dole, and her husband, an insurance broker, fell into the ranks of those who searched the columns of the 'wanted' in the papers. He had started work at the age of fourteen. By the time he was forty, when the Great War had stolen his best years, he was redundant. That security which the Edwardians had seen as the great goal of life was not to be his. None the less, with the wife's small inherited income, they managed. And with only one child, a son away at a Choir School, there was no real hardship.

But, for Lilian, there was loneliness, as the husband drifted from job to job, coming home every evening, delicately Micawberian in his manner, always hopeful for the better times which never came. The little French upright in its walnut case would fill the gap, as nothing else could. As the son became a more competent musician than his mother, he would accompany her, and urge her to sing Brahms, Schubert or Schumann. But *lieder* was beyond her, and they would return to the hackneyed ballads.

'No, son. It's no good. I can only sing the old songs.'

'But, Mother, these *are* the old songs. This sentimental stuff – can't you see how feeble it is in comparison with Schubert?'

'What's wrong with being sentimental? I *am* sentimental.'

Philip would sigh; his father look up from the pages of *John Bull*, the weekly magazine, where he worked at 'Bullets', a word competition which was then the rage. 'It won't hurt you to do what your mother asks, old chap.'

So, yet again, from Lilian's voice thoughts would take wing and the caravan would rest down in the forest. And as Philip grew older and his mother sang less frequently, retreating more and more into a defensive inner world, the 'old songs' seemed to come from the piano of their own accord, whether she sang or not.

When she died, another war had passed. The piano, now in Philip's possession, became as precious to him as it had been to the singer. Living now in Cornwall where he brought up his family and eked out a precarious existence as a painter, he would go to the keyboard in moments of doubt. Extemporising, he would recover faith in the life he had chosen – a life which had dismissed the idea of 'security' as pointless. Always he found that the piano gave him courage to go on with his work.

During the years, there were many moves, and the piano went with the family. Always kept tuned, the tone was still beautiful, although the walnut case was split. Serene and resonant, it sang of past days as remote as Cornwall was from London. Then came times when Philip had often to be away from home, and the piano was hardly touched. He would return, open the lid, play a few chords, then close it abruptly. Nobody in the family really needed the piano, and it became a reproach to Philip. When the house had to be let furnished one winter and he came back to find it had been moved into a damp room with a window left open to the sou-westerly drive of scudding rain, he felt that the end had come. For no tuner had been during the long wet winter, and what notes sounded were now wildly out. The hammers would not respond, the walnut veneer was peeling badly, some of the ivories were loose. It was only a mockery of music that came now from the little Bord. Who could want it, in its present condition?

The time came for the house to be sold, and the future was too uncertain to move the piano yet again and have it restored. Some old friends who lived in an ancient farmhouse above the western sea offered to store it for him. 'Somebody may be glad of it one day,' they said.

But seven more years passed, and now the piano, never played, stayed lodged away in a corner of a room already over-packed with furniture. Yet there was usually a fire here, so the room itself was kind to the piano. Whenever he visited the farmhouse Philip would open the lid, play a few out-of-tune notes, never daring to sound a chord. It pleased him to find that at least the piano had not suffered from its long exile in the home of his friends, two widowed sisters. 'Give it to anyone who needs it,' he said.

One day, the right person turned up – a young American girl, whose mother was a cousin of the sisters. Leila had left California longing to see Europe and research her Cornish background; and in the process, she found a husband. Julian, a long-haired Adonis who had ditched his university after two dry years of mathematics, had no idea what he wanted to do with his life. But he knew, the moment he saw Leila, deeply engrossed in a book at a café table in Montparnasse, that he wanted her. When he saw, over her shoulder, that she was read-ing Mozart's letters, he knew that they would have a common interest in music. It was an easy opening. With his guitar and husky voice and her to collect the money, they spent the summer and early autumn busking in Paris. But when the leaves drifted down from the planes and chestnuts it was time to leave.

'You must take me to Cornwall,' she said.

'Cornwall? That's way out of anywhere. We shall never earn any money there.'

But she was insistent. 'I must go. It belongs to my past. I've got to meet those sisters. They'll help us.'

So they presented themselves, out of the blue, at the farm-house; and when Leila spoke of her mother in America, they were immediately given royal treatment. A meal spread out on the huge kitchen table, blackberries and rich yellow cream, freshly baked heavycake, saffron buns, a fire blazing in the slab. The two old sisters bustled around the young couple and talked of their cousin from memories of her, long ago. Leila was entranced by it all. The place was older, more dense with the warm harmony of family treasures, in furniture, ornaments, glass paintings, clocks and cats, than she could have imagined. And in their crowded parlour, as the October rain slashed at the little windows, she saw the forlorn piano, tucked away in its corner, with framed photographs and stacks of magazines on top of it. It was the one thing that seized her attention.

'Do play something,' she asked. Then the sisters told her that neither of them played, and were only storing the piano for an old friend. And when they added that he would give it to anyone who needed it she was filled with excitement.

'We must have it, Julian. We must have it.'

'Don't be so stupid, Leila. We haven't even got a place to live.'

'That doesn't matter. The piano was meant to come to me. Don't you see?'

The sisters were greatly concerned when they realized that the young lovers had nowhere to set up home. 'If it's any use to you,' they said, 'there's a hut down in the Cott Valley. It belonged to a brother of ours who went to Australia. We've been letting it to summer visitors, but it needs so much doing to it and – '

So it was that through the piano, they found a home. For weeks Julian and Leila worked at the place, adding another room to it, using timber from a huge demolished chapel in the village, piping water from the valley stream, hacking out the furze and bramble up the hillside. Living very sparely on the money they had earned in Paris, they resorted to the unfail-ing hospitality of the farmhouse as funds began to run out. They were not really worried about the future, even when

Leila became pregnant. Now was the time to get married, they decided. They did, and social security came to the rescue.

One day in early spring an old van lumbered slowly along the narrow rutted lane leading to the hut, which had now been transformed into a three-room chalet, bearing the name, painted on it by Julian: Van Cara. The name had been found after great deliberation between them, and it was Leila who had hit on it. 'It sounds kinda Spanish. And we always said we wanted a caravan. I bet you nobody'll get what it means.'

'You're right,' said Julian. 'Anyway, your name is Persian. And so is caravan. Van Cara. Yes I do like it.'

With the help of two friends Julian dragged the piano up the last bit of hillside, fixing planks under it, pulling on ropes, heaving, pushing, swearing and sweating, while Leila watched. It was a tricky operation. Once, balanced on a slant sideways, only held by the exertion of six strong arms, the little Bord was tired enough to crash down through gorse and bramble to the rushing stream far below, and there say farewell to music. Leila wanted to help, but Julian would not let her; he was too anxious for the baby. So she stood aside, and watched them as they urged it upwards, inch by perilous inch, while Julian shouted desperate instructions. At last the piano came to its new home.

A blind tuner was found, who at once realized that he had a fine old instrument to restore. From then, day by day, the little Bord came to new life under Leila's fingers. Down the bracken-dense hillside where the stream trickled to the valley the sound of music mingled with the sound of water. The child quickened within Leila. As her time came nearer so did she play the more passionately. Sometimes she would sing, and Julian would sing with her, songs they had sung in Montparnasse where it had been easy to earn two days' food in an hour. But here there were no people ready to drop coins into a hat. Only the rustling stillness of the water, the barking of foxes at night, the cry of the curlew, the distant bourdon of the sea – and music.

'It's so lovely here, Julian,' she cried, one night. 'I never want to be anywhere else – never. Van *Cara*! I want always to be here with you, and our baby safe inside me, and music, music to keep out all the bad things in the world.'

When she spoke like this, in a kind of ecstasy, he would think – how long can it go on? For gradually he began to know that he must face up to the future. He was twenty-three, she was nineteen; and there were many days to come, days when the child would be born and grow and demand from him what he could not at present give. They could be frightening thoughts, and he would attempt to dismiss them, marvelling at his beautiful young wife, as she played. He would put his own life aside, as though it did not exist, and watch her, listening, wondering.

'Gosh, Leila! You're really together. I never knew you could play like that.'

She hardly heard him. She did not need an audience. Her mother had sent a parcel of the music she had abandoned, and now she was trying to struggle through Gershwin's 'Rhapsody in Blue'. But her small hands could not encompass the stretched chords, and she threw the music aside.

'I can't play at all,' she said. 'I need years of study. It's awful. Oh Julian, if we can just stay here – not think about the world, and earning a living, all that kind of thing, I think I could make it as a proper pianist.'

He was troubled. 'Play something quiet. Tender. Simple. Just anything out of your funny little mind.'

But that evening she would not play any more. They went to their bed, and while Julian slept she stayed awake, hearing owls in the gnarled thorns. The wind whistled round the chalet, and while it was still dark she got up, made tea, and went to the piano.

'Play something ... anything out of your funny little mind.' Did he think she was an idiot? Why couldn't he earn money and leave her alone? She did not touch the keys but went back to their bedroom and looked down at her husband, asleep in their bed. He looked happy. Why was she so disturbed in her being? The child of their love seemed already to be asking questions: what am I to be? Do you both need me? Will you love me, forever, always? *Whatever happens?*

She went back to the piano and touched one note; and from that, another note. She realized that she had fallen into the key of E flat, the major key of Chopin's most loved Nocturne, which she could play passably well. But it was not this she wanted to play. Without any harmony, a flow of slow melody emerged as her fingers moved over the old ivories, gleaming now from the milk-wash Julian had given them.

Abruptly, she stopped, and slammed down the lid. Something other than the dawning life of the child had stirred her being; something she could not explain to herself, or even understand. A tremor ran through her body, like the ripple of water when a flat stone skims along it. She returned to their bed, got in, touched her lover, and felt his arm come over to her breasts. He had not woken, but she could hear him murmur through his sleep, 'Leila, Leila, lovely Leila....'

She was lovely. She knew that. In the morning, when Julian had walked the four miles into the market town to draw the weekly dole which kept them, she looked at herself in a long mirror Julian had fixed to the wall, near the bed. Her skin was ivory, her limbs were shapely, even though with the child in her there was something grotesque about this body of hers. Grotesque – yet so richly filled, she felt as though the whole blossoming valley, now creamy white with blackthorn, was a part of herself. Into her mind then came a melody, a melody that was new to her, yet one she seemed to remember. Had it been in the night ...?

She smoothed her hands over the lid of the piano, which Julian had revarnished and polished. He had made a beautiful job of this. The wood gleamed in the light of the sun streaming from above the hillside straight on to the piano. It was late in March now, and the valley seethed with new life. In so short a time the sun would be ascendant, midsummer would torch the bonfires along the hills of Cornwall. And their child be a living creature, beginning to live a life of its own.

As she opened the lid of the piano, she trembled. Her fingers fell into the same tune she had found in the night. She made no attempt to add harmony to this flow of melody. But by now she knew the tune. It had become a part of her. It spoke to her from the piano itself.

The day passed in a strange agony of mixed feelings. She both wanted the future, and did not want it. Almost she dreaded the birth of her child. She tried to induce methods of meditation she had begun to practise; to discover a way of existing here, and now, with no reference to past or future. To lose the troubled ego and float into the great space of pure life. Yet her own mother, far away in California, got in the way. Julian got in the way. Even the unborn child ... but there she broke off her meditation. The unborn child could not be ignored. This unknown, this unique entity, was here, was present. All that was demanded of her was patience; and this she did not possess.

In Penzance, Julian collected his money, and after a session at The First and Last pub with some friends, was driven part of the way home. Now it was late afternoon and a drizzle of thin rain in the air. He realized that he had been too long away from Leila, and that he had drunk too much. He had promised to be back by mid-day; and he had broken his promise.

Lighting a cigarette, he walked up and down the high-hedged narrow winding lane going towards the valley. He wanted to call in at the farmhouse, talk to the old sisters, warm himself at their fireside. But this would be to make a false and useless escape. He asked himself angry questions. Why had he married Leila? What did 'marriage' mean? What had those 'vows' meant? How long would he be able to honour them? He wanted Leila; he still needed her. But in years to come – would he still need her, or she need him?

It was a moment of truth for him, and he did not know how to return to the chalet with the ridiculous name. Van Cara – Van Cara! It was absurd. He ought to fix wheels on the thing so that they could go from place to place, again earn their living from the streets. Then he reproached himself as he took in the beauty of the valley. So much of life's richness lay before and around him; and he did not know how to use it, how to become fused into it. Van Cara suddenly seemed like a prison.

In the chalet, the piano was alive with music. Leila had thrown aside the pieces her mother had sent and was letting her fingers do what they would. She was making music out of her 'funny little mind,' letting florid sweeps of sound fly out in chaotic arpeggios, up and down the keyboard. Never had the piano been more fluent.

Sixty-five years earlier, over the same keyboard, in a London suburb, slender fingers had moved. And Lilian had sung:

Where my caravan has rested
Flowers I leave you on the grass ...

It was the same tune that came now from the piano. As Julian slowly climbed up the hillside pathway, he stopped, unable to take another step forward. The sound of this music filled him with joy; yet despair threatened this joy. The present moment was so wonderful; how could one black out the future? Leila's music expressed it all – his feelings of elation and guilt, of joy and despair. The world was both wonderful – and horrible. What part had he to play in it? Must he be 'up and doing' – and if so, doing what?

Diminuendo. The music had rushed away from arpeggios to a single thread of melody, supported now by a simple harmony. Leila had made the foundation for the tune. And as she played, she began to sing, without words, in a low quiet voice.

He waited, near the door. Then suddenly there was a snap in his mind. Reaching down, he plucked up from their stems a cluster of daffodils growing wild in the clefts of rock. The flowers were hateful to him. They represented life, new life, spring, all springs, and told him that all springs lead to autumn; and winter.

Leila stopped playing. The door had been flung open. Julian stood there, his face white, his hands clutched round the flower stems.

'Here's a present for you!' The flowers came in a scatter of blurred sunshine across the room, and some fell on the keyboard. His voice rang out, wild and desperate. 'That's all I've

got for you, Leila. Flowers. Just flowers. And that's all there'll
ever be. Flowers. . . .'

She sat very still, her head bowed over the keyboard. She
saw the long green stalks, the milky-white moisture, the
crushed flowers, on the keys. There was a silence. Julian
looked at her as she still sat there, her silky dark brown hair
drooping down over the keys. Then, very slowly, her fingers
moved. With no supporting harmony, the melody emerged. It
came very quietly; yet, to Julian, it was almost like a defiant
shout into the silence.

Then she stopped and slowly turned her eyes towards him.
The late sun sent a glow over his head. She smiled.

'You look wonderful,' she said. 'There, in the sun. I shall call
you Sunshine.'

'What is that tune?' he asked. His voice was thick, choked
with self-anger.

'What is that tune, dear?'

In the London suburb, Lilian's husband, returning from a
bad day in the city when he had been told that his firm was
closing down in a week's time, stood in the doorway of the
brown brick house. He could not bear to bring her bad news.

'Oh that!' Lilian sniffed in her scornful manner. 'It's a new
song – "Where my caravan has rested".'

'The piano sounds lovely.' He put his neat bowler hat on the
hatstand and laid his paper and umbrella on the hall chair. He
was tired. But it had been good to hear his young wife singing
and playing the piano he had given her.

'It's a good piano,' said Lilian. 'I wish I could play it better.
But thank you, dear. Thank you for it.'

She sat on the chair in the hallway, looking lost and yet
grand. He was touched to see her sitting thus, so defenceless.
He wondered when he would be able to tell her his bad news.
Not yet, he thought; not yet.

'Had a good day?' she asked. She knew he had not.

'Up and down,' he said. He hummed a little tune. 'You know
how it is. But the weather – never been lovelier, has it? Everybody was saying in the City – we've never had a spring like it.'

'There's a letter from Philip,' she said. 'He's coming on well with his music.'

And as she spoke and he looked at her, so mysteriously sitting there, looking lost and faraway in their suburban home they would soon have to leave for a cheaper one, she felt as though she had glided away into some other country.

'What *is* that tune? You were playing it in the night.'

'Sunshine, darling. I don't know. But it's nice, isn't it? It kinda grew from my funny little mind.'

'No,' said Julian. 'It didn't grow from you. From the piano.'

Going to the keyboard, he carefully picked up the half crushed flowers, moulded them all in the palms of his hands, then dropped the moist remains before her.

'You're together,' he said. 'You're really together. I'm not. I wish I were.'

Late that night Julian was polishing the wood of the piano. 'This thing has had a long life behind it,' he said. 'And I reckon it's got plenty of life before it.'

As he spoke, in a beam of moonlight Lilian floated away from the chalet, and merged into the dark and streaming richness of the spring life in the valley. Leila felt the same tremor ripple over her body.

'That moonlight!' she cried, 'It's alive. It's really alive!'

Going to the piano, she tried to find the melody that had dissolved their problems. But she had lost it.

'It doesn't matter,' she said. 'It's the kind of thing you remember when you get quite old.'

But the piano still contained the song.

IX

Coombe Morwen

It's almost dark. It has taken me over an hour to copy most of what Morgan Foster wrote, here at Coombe Morwen. I have to admit to myself (there's nobody else here to admit to) that I wish I was back in my dreary but warm bedsitter in Exeter and had never come out here at all today. Certainly I would not have stayed to copy this extraordinary outpouring had I not realised I'd missed the three-thirty bus and was left with a three hour wait before me. I wish now I'd shoved the thing back to the keeper and gone for a walk. And now it's raining. I find it hard to remember clearly the early part of this afternoon, I've been so engrossed in Foster's story.

Here I am at St Breward's. The Folk Museum has become a kind of a haunt of mine for the last few months, ever since my stay in Exeter. I wanted to make a last visit before I leave Devon next week. More than the exhibits in the old manor it was the cottages and farmhouses reconstructed in the grounds which fascinated me – and this one more than the others. Coombe Morwen, a seventeenth-century farmhouse. More 'atmosphere', I thought – though maybe this was really due to the keeper who fastened on to me at once, God knows why. I never liked him, with his slow way of speaking, his heavy awkward body, ingratiating manner. And the limp. Something wrong with his right leg which makes him drag it about as though it weren't part of him. He's been here for years, I'm told, and I can't imagine him anywhere else. Certainly Foster got him all right.

Today, I made straight for the house. It lies near a spinney, far from the manor. I had a bit of a problem, I wanted a quiet place to chew it over, and this seemed to be it. But the keeper wasn't going to have this. The moment I appeared on the scene he must have said, 'Here he comes; I've got him.' (God! How like poor Foster that sounds!) Although I wandered from room to room to try to escape, this only served to emphasise my interest in the house and its time-worn furniture. It was in the small cold kitchen – a very dark room – where he finally nailed me.

I was looking at an exhibit new here since my last visit. Amongst the butter-mixers, flour bins, copper saucepans, other friendly domestic chattels, this had a grating incongruity which cast a shadow over the slumbering peace of the old place.

'Ah. That's the mantrap, sir.'

He had limped up behind me. I did not turn round, only murmured I was aware of it. A notice attached to the black chains of the grisly iron contraption told me what it was.

'Punishing things, sir.'

I agreed it was punishing, and turned as though to go back to the comparative warmth of the living-room, where a wood fire burned. But he went on.

'It's part of the house, you might say, though it was found in the old barn. They decided to bring it here. Of course, it wouldn't have been kept in the kitchen, sir; not the sort of thing they'd want the children to see, if there were any children. No. Out in the woods you'd have stepped on it, if you'd been a poacher. And I don't suppose you'd forget that step for a long time.'

I said it was odd that the authorities should bring such a diabolical device to the peace of Coombe Morwen.

'Odd, sir? Maybe. I always think poor Foster's case had something to do with that.'

I asked who 'poor Foster' was.

'Gone now, sir; so I'm at liberty to talk about him. Morgan Foster, a journalist chap, worked on the *Exeter Guardian*, about thirty-five he was when he first got into the way of coming here. I took to him at once, I did. Like yourself, sir, I could see this old place meant something more to him that it meant to most. And he kept it all to himself, too; never told a soul of his visits here. Even his sister, Adelaide – she never knew. I got to know Miss Foster, you see, sir, after he'd been put away; I felt sorry for her, like. I don't know what it is, but I'm sympathetic to other people's troubles. I reckon I convinced him I really was his friend those times I went to see him afterwards, whenever I could manage it. That must have been why he gave me what he'd written here.'

I remembered nothing of Foster, not being a native of Exeter. But making a mental note that he had been 'put away' I asked the keeper what it was he had written here.

It might have been the question he was asking for.

'I'll show you, sir. What you'll make of it, I don't know. But you mustn't take no notice of what he says about me. Confused, that's what he was. No wonder too, with what he had on his mind, or what was left of it.'

We went back to the living-room. From a little oak cabinet he took a grubby students' exercise book. Then he pointed to a gatebacked chair by the heavy oak table, under the low four-paned window.

'You read that, sir. Read it where he wrote it.'

It must have been then that a man's voice called from the garden, startling in the quietness.

'Tom, they dam' sheep are all over your garden.'

The keeper called back. 'Coming, Joe.' And he went to the door.

'I'll leave you to peruse that, sir. I know it's safe with you.'

I felt flattered. Sitting at the table I lit a cigarette and opened the notebook. The earlier pages are clearly and carefully written. Once I had started I had to read on. And now I shall read again what Foster wrote and what I have just copied, in the place where he wrote it.

'I must describe the house. It is an L-shaped farmhouse with a dark pink distemper wash and a weight of heavy thatch on the roof. It once stood in a remoter countryside of north Devon, and was taken down, beam by numbered beam, stone by numbered stone, and rebuilt as one of the specimen houses in the estate of St Breward. The greatest care has gone into the reconstruction of Coombe Morwen, as far as possible all the original material being used. Each room has the furniture of its period and even came with the house, so that when you step over the threshold you take a long step back – into the past. I was drawn to it from the first time I saw it and was shown over it by the keeper, who seemed to regard it as his own place. I often came on summer days when many other visitors trailed in and out; and I began to want to be alone here.

'The day I am writing about, that day in November, I *was* alone, and had a great need to be. I had guessed that here at Coombe Morwen, with only the keeper for company, I could come to terms with myself. I was deeply in trouble; but of that I am not going to write. I had returned to the house to take stock of myself, thinking I could do it more easily here.

'As I approached the solitude of the house and saw the woodsmoke from its chimney ascending towards the cold bloom of the winter sky, my troubles seemed to recede with every footstep. I remember I hurried, as though time and the falling sun would cheat me of my objective – whatever that was.

'But I must make it clear. I am writing this in Coombe Morwen itself, three weeks after the visit I intend to describe; and I must make it clear also that I do not think I am ever likely to be able to put this place behind me. Nobody will mind my being here, that is certain; even the summer visitors will hardly notice me. By then I shall be a part of the place, a fixture, numbered like stones and beams. The keeper seems to know this; he glances at me now, then looks away, pretending I do not exist. I must accept this, I know I must accept it. But I would like.... There are moments when I want to get away and back again – or should I say 'forward' again? – to the world of movement which still drones on, in the City. But I must stay, stay here; this is my world. As I sit writing on the polished oak table, dark in a room sweet and heavy with the scent of straw, beeswax and woodsmoke, I feel myself going back to that first winter visit, when the others came into my life, or I into theirs

– I don't, even now, know which way round it should be. The keeper knows. But not for anything would I ask him. I must be careful what I say to him. He is quite near me now. Let him wait. He is fulfilled, like a monk with his silence. He has me.'

(Here, Foster leaves a blank of half a page. Then:)

'Unlike today, three weeks ago was clear, and glittering with frost. But now a grey mist swarms up from the river bed, the air is humid and dank, nothing has solidity. As I write, sitting under the small window to catch the last of the afternoon's meagre light, I try to catch back the feel, the growing pressure of the other visit. Sometimes I stop and look around me, searching for a word; and I know that the keeper is watching me. If I were to go through the cold little kitchen to the back door, he would be there; and if I were to go to the front door, he would be there.

'I remember his first words, last time. "So you've come back to us, sir."

'It was not a question; it was a statement. "Yes," I agreed, "I've come back. I wanted to get the feel of the place, with nobody else here – alone, you understand?"

'Perhaps my voice was strained, for the trouble I have mentioned was heavy on my mind.

'He repeated my words. "The feel of the place? Ah. You'll get that all right, sir."

'I wanted to lose him. So I said, "Well.... now I've got it to myself, at least I assume so. Nobody else here, is there?"

'"I've been here a long time, sir; and I wouldn't rightly say you ever have Coombe Morwen to yourself."

'Then he moved away to the room at the back, adjoining the kitchen, leaving me to what little heat came from the fire of ash logs which smouldered on the stone hearth, where sullen smoke was drawn up the deep well of the gaping chimney. And after a little while I heard, as I expect to hear again, the whispering.

'First, the woman. I remember, just before, the hissing of a crumbling log and a last filter of weak sun drifting down into the dusty silence. I remember the western sun and the comforting log because neither are here now. It is all mist outside, and the fire sluggish, with a wounded red ruin at its heart.

'It is difficult to go on writing. For I am trying to remember the whispering and listen for it to come again. I must be very quiet. . . .

'I stopped writing. For one half minute I stopped, timing it by my watch, the watch Adelaide gave me for my twenty-first birthday. I let thirty seconds chase themselves away. And now I ask myself – why am I writing this? Who am I writing it for? Is it because I want to communicate something of— No. Nothing of that must come into it. I came to Coombe Morwen today only to check up, only to note a few details, only – yes, that's all.

'No good pretending. Not true. I came, because I had to come, because nothing could have stopped me. In the *Guardian* office where I worked, there is an empty desk. I am always aware of that vacant place; I hear people asking – what has happened to Morgan Foster? They may never know the truth, yet I want them to know I am here, and why I had to come here.

'I am calmer, having written that. And now I can put down, quite objectively, what I heard whispered.

'"He has come then?" Those were the four words. At first they hardly penetrated my mind.

'A man's voice answered the woman. "Yes. He has come."

'It was then that I thought – the keeper has lied to me. There are others in the house. And then I remembered – the keeper had never said there was nobody else. His phrase had been, "I wouldn't rightly say you ever have Coombe Morwen to yourself."

'I got up and moved very quietly to the door of the other room. It was half open, and in the gloom I could see the keeper, standing with his back to me, solid and still, his hands behind him playing with a length of picture cord. He was facing a blackened chimney corner, where an old spit hung unturning and no fire burned. I could see nothing of the woman. Yet it seemed that it was from a stool, below the keeper, that her voice came.

'"What makes you so sure he is the right one?"

'It was his answer which I can never forget – those words which drove me to action and gave me freedom, of a kind, from the burden I carried and carry no more; and words which drew me back here today to play out the rest of the scene.

'"Because he desires what I desire and is prepared to be damned for it. Because I said that not till this one came would I do what I have to do. And now he has come, and I am ready."

'"What do you desire, brother?"

'When she called him "brother" I knew of a certainty that I had been caught into action beyond any control. In my mind I had sought justification for what I wanted to do; and this was it – a double justification, for him, for me.

'He spoke again. (And when I write 'he' I do not mean it was the keeper, although the keeper was standing there.)

'"You know what I desire. Coombe Morwen is yours, father left it all to you. You know well what I desire."

'Yes, I knew too – oh, so well!

'He went on. "You have poisoned my life, sapped my manhood, driven your rot into my soul."

'She spoke again, bitter, pitiful. "I am sick. Who have I got but you?"

'His voice rose, thick with passion. The whole house seemed to tremble with it.

' "Yes, you are sick. Sick of a disease you call love. But you could never love any man but me, the man from the same womb. I tried to get away from you. I left Coombe Morwen and went to sea. Then father died, and you were ill, so I came back to nurse you. And you had the house and the land; but you were never content, you must have me as well. You wanted to lock us both away from the world. You made me lover, not brother. You even desire children by me.'

'I saw the keeper (if it was the keeper) bring his hands sharply before his body, with the picture cord twined round his fingers. And my fingers were dry, on edge. I could hardly bear to touch the rough tweed of my coat. I heard him speak the words which sealed me.

'"I shall kill you."

'She drew in her breath, gasping, as if already she were choking. My fingers were curled and tensed, I was paralysed. He went on:

'"They will find the poacher with money on him, money I shall take from you. I have set the mantrap by the wood. He will be blamed, not me. He will take my punishment. And Coombe Morwen will be mine."

'"I shall always be here with you, brother. Always. Always. Always here."

'"Go up to bed. I shall bring you your posset. And after, when you settle for sleep...."

'He did not finish the sentence. Yes, I thought – when she settled for sleep. That was the time....

'Her voice came once more, and now from the foot of the stairs, yet far away, as if from the end of a long tunnel.

'"Listen, brother. I make you a prophecy. If this house is taken down and moved to another place, then, and only then will you lay your hands on me. But the house can never be moved."

'When he answered, it seemed that I answered with him.

'"The house has been moved to another place. We have come with it. I have waited only for him to come, and he is here now."

'That was all I heard. And then, in the silence, the keeper turned round and faced me.

'"Everything all right, sir?"

'I said yes – yes, everything was as it should be, and now I am calm, like a last leaf on an autumn tree, knowing I must drift to earth, but not yet. As I write now the same sense of relief fills me. I listen again for further words; nothing comes. Why should it? I was shown the way, I have taken it. The way, the truth and the death? Is it that? It doesn't matter. I can smoke and relax now. The keeper is about the place. I feel easy. Perhaps I shall go up and celebrate. I am very calm, with a greater calm than I have had in these three weeks, ever since I closed the door of our house in St Andrew's Street, and knew that Adelaide might stay there, undisturbed, for months.

'Yes. I am calm. I feel safe here. I knew I should be safe here, when I came today. For it is my place. Coombe Morwen. Mine.'

I've read what I've copied so far, and it makes me ask a lot of questions. Too many, and uncomfortable ones. I suppose, if I were staying on in Exeter, I might be tempted to follow up two things: the actual circumstances of Foster's life with his sister, Adelaide; and what is known about the history of Coombe Morwen. And – the background of the keeper who still leaves me to myself here.

There's still an hour to go before the bus, and it's bloody cold here. I'd better copy the rest of Foster's stuff, though I begin to wish I'd never embarked on it at all. The next bit is much more incoherent, words scribbled rapidly, harder to read. It looks as though he were scaring himself as he wrote, which isn't any wonder –

Here's the last of it, then.

'I have done what I never meant to do, I have, I have written about her. If anyone reads –

'Burn it all in the fire – burn it – *no*. Go on writing, *go on*. The keeper has got used to you writing here – here – here. Always, she said ... Always. She would always be here. Of course, I knew that when I came back today. Accept. Curiously calming, just to know there's no escape. If you can't escape, you're safe, that stands to reason. All you have to do is repeat it, repeat it, again and again, repeat it, repeat –

'The front door is opening, Someone coming in. It is very dark now, you will not be seen. Somebody coming towards me – must be the keeper, must be –

'"Do you answer to the name of Morgan Foster of 17 St Andrew's Street, Exeter?"'

'I have written that down, just as he said it. Don't answer.
Don't look up. Safe here.... always....'

Then follows a statement which, unlike the above, seems quite
controlled. It was written, the keeper tells me, later on the
same day, in the Police Station.

'This is the statement of Morgan Foster, of 17 St Andrew's
Street, Exeter. I have said I will not answer questions. I will
state what I have to state here, where I have been brought
under duress, and charged with an act of violence against my
sister, Adelaide. I have been told that she has been sent for, to
come and see me here. If this is so, I will not recognise her, I
refuse to admit that I have failed. But before I discuss this further I wish to explain why I lost control of myself on the edge
of the wood near Coombe Morwen, when I made an attempt
to run away from the policeman who had charge of me. It was
the mantrap. I think it was wrong of them to place it there.
When I saw the square iron platform half concealed by dead
bracken with the spiked teeth gaping open ready to snap I lost
command of myself. I now wish that I had planted my foot
firmly on that platform, for if it had any life left in it I think I
could more have endured the pain of being held by that than
the pain which holds me now. I realise now, of course, that the
thing had long been out of use, and had only been put there
as an exhibit, in the kind of place it would have been. But I
do not think it should have been left there, and I am sorry it
caused me to give so much trouble. The policeman who led
me away was kind enough. He cannot have understood that I
could feel the teeth meeting in the flesh of my leg. And I do
not expect anyone to understand that what gnaws at me now
is worse. She said – as in what I have written of what I heard
at Coombe Morwen – she said he would live with it forever;
and this is right for me too. When I went back to the house
today I felt certain it was all behind me, forever finished; but it
is too close behind me, and it can never be finished. Perhaps I
shall be allowed to return to Coombe Morwen when I freely
confess that I killed my sister, Adelaide, three weeks ago, after

the visit to the house I have described. It will be seen from this
that I had to do what I did, and I will not believe I failed. I had
to do it, not just because she made a hell of my life but also
because I had to act within the inevitable design showed to
me at Coombe Morwen. If the house had not been moved this
could not have happened; but the house was moved, therefore
it had to happen, and I am not responsible.

'The Inspector who was watching me here as I write has
gone out, and now he is returning with someone else. It is a
woman. I will not look at her. She is now standing right close
to me. I hear her words. "Oh Morgan, how could you? And
you – all I had." But now she has not got me, not as she had me
before. It does not matter if I failed, for the desire is all important, and I made the essential action. I feel strong. I can live
with my hatred. Nothing can change me. Whatever they do to
me, it does not matter. It does not – Christ! I looked at her. In
only three weeks she has aged greatly. Yet she looks as though
she will never die. . . .'

'Yet she looks as though she will never die.' According to the
keeper he never added any more, or made any verbal statement, either in the police station, or later.

Less and less do I feel like making any comment on all this,
and I wish to God I'd never copied it. But there is still time on
my hands and while today is fresh in my mind I might as well
write the end of the matter, as far as I'm concerned – if I am
concerned. And in some way I am.

The keeper, as I've noted, went out to see to the sheep, leaving me to read Foster's mad ramblings. After my first reading
of it – that is, before I'd made this copy – he hadn't returned.
I heard a scuttling sound in the other room, something tiny
rustling across the flagstones. I went in, but couldn't discover
any reason for the sound at first; then I saw it moving – nothing but a dead, dried leaf on the floor, blown in with a sudden
gust of wind. I picked it up, and looked at the mantrap. There
it stood like an outsize gin, reminding me that men had once
been treated like rats.

I stood there for a few seconds, uncertain whether to leave the place now, and wait for the bus by the village church. But it would be a long wait and it was still raining. Then it was that I heard another sound, upstairs, a board creaking and a kind of muffled thump. Going to the foot of the bare polished stairway, I called. No answer. So I went up.

Nobody there, which didn't surprise me. But I looked into the two main bedrooms, lofty rooms with a weight of thatch bunched above the ancient double beds, one of them a four-poster. I thought of beds and what they meant to us – begetting, birth, death. The door to the little room, often closed to visitors because of some loose boards, was open. I went to it. There was a shelving step down and I almost fell and had to clutch the door lintel.

I heard four words spoken. They were, in fact, 'Be careful now, sir.' But as I write this I think of four other words. 'He has come then.'

It was, of course, the keeper. He came towards me, putting his hand out to my arm. But I signified I had no need for his help. For some reason I didn't want him to touch me.

'I didn't hear you come up,' I said. 'I was lost in what you gave me to read.'

He said he had come the back way, and asked me, 'How did you take it then, sir?'

I asked him whether Foster had been right as to the history of the house. 'As near as could be,' he said, 'though he never got it from me.' In 1790, it appears, the last of a family called Price lived here, a brother and sister, Hubert and Dorcas. Hubert ran away to sea, and his father disowning him, left house and land to the daughter and died before Hubert returned. He found that in his absence his sister had virtually starved the mother to death, to get possession of the place. Hubert tried to strangle Dorcas, but failed, and was caught in the mantrap he had set for the poacher.

'It was said in Morwenbeare that he was held there for two whole days, sir, his leg mangled horrible. Dorcas Price heard his screams, they say – but would she go to him? Not that lady!

Found by the squire's men he was, and all the money taken from the house where she'd hoarded it — in that little cabinet downstairs, sir — crushed into the ground where he'd been stamping and struggling with his one free foot. Better, I say, to have left him, instead of dragging him out to hang him, which they did.'

I asked him whether there had been an incestuous relationship.

'Well, sir, all we know for certain — because he's in the Parish register — is that she had a child, but nobody knew who the father was. She hid the poor little thing from the villagers, and when he died — it was in this room, sir — she didn't last long. And that was the end of the Price family.'

I looked at the crumbling old bed, covered by a tattered patchwork quilt.

'After that,' he went on, 'various folk took on Coombe Morwen, but never any luck nobody had, till, in 1933, it stood empty and rotting away for three years. Then the trustees of St Breward's got it, and here it is, sir, for all to visit. I expect Mr Foster dug the story out somehow and that's why he took to coming here, his being a similar tale, like.'

'But how similar?' I asked him sharply. I doubted every word the man said by now. 'For example, was there any such relationship between him and his sister?'

'Well, sir ... There was something — not quite as it should be, you felt. And she went on visiting him, every day, at the East Devon Infirmary, and that can't have been exactly a comfort. Detained at His Majesty's pleasure, sir, see? The doctors tried to do what they could for him. But he never opened his mouth, except once or twice when she failed to turn up. Then he'd go raving mad, attacked the nurses sometimes. Oh, very difficult, he could be then, very difficult! I could calm him down a bit; and I reckon he appreciated that, in his dumb way. Anyway, he said several times that he wanted me to have his notebook, it ought to be at Coombe Morwen, he said. The police had let him have it back, you see, sir; one of the doctors had suggested it might help him to have it. It was quoted at the Assize by his counsel, every bit of it read out. But Foster, never one more word did he say, except he pleaded guilty. Four years in that place, then he went and died, quiet like. I went to the funeral, sir – and the only one, me and Miss Foster. I often think, must have been terrible for him to know he'd failed, like the other one before him, or alongside of him, as you might say. You see, sir, when he comes up here that November day he writes about, he really did think he'd gone for her; a strangling job, see? But he hadn't got very strong hands, very delicate they were. Then he locks up the house, leaving her unconscious, and spends three weeks in the Albany Hotel in Exeter, living on money he'd taken from Miss Foster. Of course he had the wits to use another name.

'Then one day, December the 21st, he comes back here again. And that was his undoing, because a policeman sees him get on the bus for St Breward's, and follows. He hadn't once left the Albany in that three weeks. Then his cash runs out, and he comes back here, to take stock of himself, like he says in his book. Miss Foster, she screamed the house down when she came round, till the neighbours called the police and they find her, locked in her bedroom. She still had the marks of it round her neck, even when I met her. Act of violence! I should say it was! But she forgave him, and never gave up hope she'd get him back home with her. Better, I sometimes think, if he'd gone the way of Hubert Price; more merciful than to spin out the rest of his days as he did – seeing her every day, too.'

(And, I thought, at times the keeper.)

I made a move towards the stairhead; but he was barring the door with his lumbersome body. I asked why the mantrap had been left outside on the edge of the wood.

He looked at me. He had pinkish bland eyes.

'That, sir? It never was left outside. He imagined that, like his voices. What happened was – the copper comes, finds him writing downstairs where you were sitting, can't get a word out of him, takes him in charge and leads him out. Then, sudden, he makes a run for it, and when he gets to the edge of the wood he begins to scream – terrible sound it was, cut right

across to the old barn, quarter mile away, where I was talking
to Joe – him who got me out to the sheep just now. Terrible
sound.'

'The barn?' I looked steadily at him. 'But you were here, in
the house. He keeps referring to you.'

'Oh no, sir. I told you there were things he got wrong about
me, and that was one of them, as I said in court when I had to
give evidence. I was never in the house at all that afternoon.
Burning leaves, near the barn, I was. Here the first time he
writes about I might have been. But never that day. Oh no!
Never even saw him come. Only heard him screaming later.
Never forgot that. Nobody could.'

It was then, foolishly, I asked whether I could borrow Foster's narrative to make a copy; I felt it was too strange a story
to lose.

But he wouldn't have this. 'I couldn't let it out of my
care, sir. It's a kind of sacred trust, like everything else what's
come to roost here. But you're welcome to copy it now, on
the premises. I can make the fire up for you and come back
in half-an-hour or so. I've got to see all the other houses are
locked up for the night.'

I remarked that it would take me some time to copy it. But
he made light of this. 'Your time's your own, sir. And I've got
paper here; I'm making some notes myself about the place,
little bit of amateur research, like.'

At last he limped down the stairs, and I followed. My mind
was racing. I did not want to stay. Yet now I had missed the bus
and. . . .

He found paper, bellowsed up the fire, lit a candle and went
to the door. 'Make yourself comfortable, sir. Take your time.
No hurry. Time's what we make of it, that's what I always say.'

Then he went.

And still no sign of him. Not that I want to see him. But there's
a lot I'd like to get out of him. There's something monstrous,
something forced, about all this; something too inhuman to be
real – the whole story seems distorted. But if it is, by whom?

Foster? He sounds pathetic. I feel that his story had been blown up out of all proportion – though certainly you could say, taking his writing at its face value, that if he hadn't come here he might never have tried to kill his sister – if he even did so. Is the whole thing an obsessive fiction of the keeper's? But no – he could not have written what I have copied. Yet, if Foster had never met him. . . .

Is this where it is rooted then, in the keeper? – a disease which he holds here, to infect suitable victims? Murder unresolved – the thought never consummated in the act: a darker hell than murder itself. . . .

I'd better go. No good waiting longer for him. Yet there's still twenty minutes before the bus, and I feel I ought to check on some details of that vile mantrap. But I don't; I stay, looking down at the table, and all I have written. I wait for the sound of his uneven footsteps outside in the half dusk. But all I hear is the steady fall of rain, rain gushing down now.

I think of Foster, four years inside, and his sister visiting him every day. I suppose, in his mind, he was always here – *is* always here. And Hubert Price, and Dorcas, Adelaide – always here at Coombe Morwen, with their keeper. . . .

Always here. . . .

That bloody leaf is scuttling across the flagstones in the kitchen again. I must get out of this place. . . .

X

Tyme Tryeth Troth

The field was very wide and the path twisted across it towards a tall stone hedge. Above the hedge the man could see the chimneys and the two top windows of a cottage, and as from one of the chimneys there was smoke, he assumed that the place was occupied. The path seemed to lead to some flat stone jutting out like steps from the hedge, and it would only bring him, he reflected, into the garden of the cottage. But peasant people would not mind him passing through; and he could ask them the nearest way back to the village.

The evening was October and the rose colours of sunset were dawning in the sky. He could smell wood-smoke as he drew nearer to the stone hedge, and looking to the window of one of the upper rooms he saw the face of a small child pressed against the pane.

He smiled, pleased by the picture. He was reminded of those old glass paintings which he liked to collect; and he had a momentary sensation that he was seeing the picture the wrong way round, not looking at the reverse side of the design which was meant to be seen but at the crude blobs on the back of the glass which were not meant to be seen – except by the crafts-man himself. Then the child moved, and at the same time the sun burnt in the window and the image was dissolved into a shivering chord of fire.

His foot was on the lowest stone jutting from the hedge. And now his other foot touched the second step and he pulled himself up with an effort, feeling suddenly very tired although he had walked only a couple of miles from the sea. Tired and curiously anguished; burdened with matters he could not understand; an unhappy man searching for home, and hardly able to drag his body up to the hedge top.

He realized in those few seconds while he was climbing how intensely unhappy and desperate he had become, how much his soul longed for peace, how weary he was of being alone, and how futile his efforts to make happiness his child had become. A scruff of beard made this man look much older than he was; and the hand, rather yellow and wrinkled, that now touched the patch of grass on the hedge was more like the hand of an old man than a young one.

And all these hopeless feelings were centralized in a point of bitter envy for the inmates of the cottage on the other side who, he guessed, were happier than he was. For there was a child; there was smoke in the autumn sky; and (he noticed this suddenly as he drew himself up to the top) there was a woman in one of the downstairs rooms, sitting below a small table, writing, her hair as gold as the leaves that now began to drift from the trees, hanging loosely and obscuring her features. A wood fire was alive in the grate near her.

He watched her, deeply fascinated. Her attitude was so full of unconscious beauty, she was so completely wrapped up in whatever she was writing (perhaps a letter to her mother, he thought); she was so living and natural a part of her surroundings, he could not imagine her anywhere else but in that room, with the generous autumn fire burning yet never consuming its fuel.

And then, with a sudden shock, he realized he was not the only person watching her. Some way back from the window stood a man, a saw in his hand. There were many sawn logs of wood by the open cottage door, an old wicker basket twined with a green decoration; and on one of the logs a small white kitten played with its tail. This man, too, was watching the woman, very intently, with a happy reflective smile; a young man, clean-shaven, wearing only an open shirt and corduroy trousers, and looking full of that natural and beautiful tiredness which comes of physical labour.

The trespasser felt suddenly that he had committed an

unforgivable sin. It was not possible to talk to this man and thus to break in upon what was so obviously a touching family reverie. The wife busy with her letter; the child, supposed to be in bed upstairs, who had climbed to the window-seat to watch his father sawing wood and to see the sun slide the day away; the husband pausing in his work to survey his treasure and to wonder at the beauty of his wife – all this had a significance that meant much to the traveller. He was a very sensitive man and he dared not break in upon their peace; for he feared that his own unhappiness would infect them and leave a mark of disquietude in the air.

And the man had not seen him. It was still possible to retreat before he should turn round. Perhaps the child might have seen him; but he would be too young to relate it. The picture of this visitor who had paused on the hedge top would drift deep down into the child's memory and one day, perhaps many years hence, float up to the surface like a rising tendril of weed in spring water.

Quickly he jumped back into the field, extremely anxious now not to be observed. Right back across that long field he hurried, the day hurrying with him and night calling a full moon up from the fir trees across the downs. Presently he was on the main road and walking back towards the Trevelyan Arms, where he lodged.

After he had had supper and was in the bar, drinking with one or two local people whom he knew slightly, it occurred to him to ask who lived in the cottage. But being bad at describing places he could make no one understand exactly where it stood. There were so many cob-and-plaster cottages like that. 'A mass of tree lupins in the garden,' he explained, 'and a young family, with a small boy – at least, I think it was a boy.' But there were many families with small boys. Where was this cottage, he was again asked. He could offer no precise guide to it and so the subject was dropped.

Thinking of that happy family, he sat till the bar closed, drinking beer, and looking, without noticing it, at an account of the Trevelyans, extracted from some old antiquarian journal and framed above the bar. It was a Trevelyan who had escaped on his white horse from the devouring wave that had lost Lyonesse under the sea. A glove was in their arms. And the family motto was printed in large gothic lettering at the end of the article: Tyme Tryeth Troth.

Tyme Tryeth Troth ... The words rang the bells of memory in his mind, and repeated them lazily to himself as he sat there in the quiet bar. It had turned two, and the landlord, with whom he had become very friendly in the past few weeks, wanted to close the house. The bar was empty but for him, and he, in a happy and thoughtful mood, had fallen half asleep over his midday pint of beer. And in his dreaming he had retraced his steps across that field ten years ago, a walk that had ended in the bar where he now sat, though there had then been a different landlord and the house had not been in so smart condition as it was now. But the outline of the fortunes of the Trevelyan family had still hung on the wall, in the same corner, below a faded photograph of the village football eleven taken in 1913; and as he looked at it now he realized how deeply the words had become engraved on the tablet of his mind ... engraved like lovers' names in an old tree-trunk, obscured by the weather of many years, yet never lost.

He read a modern version of the motto: Time Testeth the Truth. And considering the wisdom of this statement – of the human and the universal meaning contained in both – he said goodbye to his friend the landlord and wandered out into the October sunshine. He was a composer and, wanting to think out the form of a new work, he had told his wife he would go for a long walk that afternoon. She would expect him back towards sunset.

But instead of the actual shape and colour of his music he found himself alive only to thoughts concerning himself, the woman he had married four years ago, and the son that had been born to them. Soon there would be another child and his life would grow more complicated. It was hard to keep his mind clear and faithful to the work he knew lay within him to do, when the demands of others, now dependent upon him, had, above everything else, to be met. He was certain that he was happier now than he had ever been; but to live firmly upon that knowledge was no easier.

He walked to the sea, and then along the coast, and rested by a fringe of tamarisks over feather waves that brushed the quiet shore. He watched shag and cormorant over the grey-gold sea where the sun enriched the water as it fell; they flew so close to the surface that it seemed as though they were chained to a submarine self who floated beneath them.

He thought how strange it was, though not in one sense at all strange, that he should have come to live for a time in that same cottage which had so much attracted him years ago; not strange, because the unknown family he had that evening for a moment studied had fixed his mind upon a destiny which for him, he had then realized, was meant to be his. And strange, because at a time when he had brought his wife and child to the West in search of somewhere to live, that particular cottage should have been empty.

Yet this all fitted into a pattern and had never surprised him; for on that first evening when he had walked to the cottage and had so hurriedly jumped back again into the field for fear of breaking in upon another's peace he had known instinctively that he would come to live here; and that he would find and bring the one true lover whose troth would be plighted with his: whose truth, united with his, would resist the tricks of time. And, after all these years, he had come: the troth was plighted eternally; time had, and certainly would again and again, test this indisputable union of flesh and spirit whose validity lay open for all to see in a son; and he was – he knew it – happy.

Yet – 'Again and again,' he murmured as the sun toured slowly across the sky. Again and again time would test them. This very evening, perhaps. One had to be for ever on guard. However firm the link uniting them, there was, just precisely because of that link, a constant tug to snap it. Cruel and sharp and saddled with resentment these divisions had been, some too terrible to be remembered. It must happen no more, he told himself; never again. She was too beautiful, too secure in her universe, too serene in her inner detachment ever again to be submitted to the bitter misery of his own rebel self.

And now he had walked again across that field and was climbing the hedge, and only realized how tired and hungry he was, with no conclusions reached regarding the music he wished to write, and the sun setting in the clear autumn sky. She had lit a fire. He could see her through the window of the sitting-room, sitting by the small table with the remains of tea scattered round her, writing a letter. Probably to her mother, he said to himself. Then he jumped down into the garden in a curiously excited way. Near the open door were logs of wood, and a basket with green twine circling its rim.

On the ground was his saw, left where he had thrown it down that morning. He stooped to pick it up, then stood with it in his hand, staring at the window where the red firelight leapt in the lower room. For a moment it seemed to him that he was struggling to remember something, to recall an instantaneous image which had flashed in and out of his mind. He felt tormented by a question, and he did not know precisely what the question was.

Suddenly he turned his head to the hedge, thinking he had heard somebody there. He climbed to the top and looked across the field; but it was empty, very long and broad, with the greenhouses at one end shivering in the vivid colour of the sun. Then he turned back to look at the cottage and saw a white kitten, their own, sitting on a bit of wood by the open door and playing with its tail.

Upstairs, from one of the windows, came a tapping sound. He looked up and saw the little boy standing in the window-seat, trying to attract his attention with a cotton-reel he was tapping on the glass. For some reason he could not respond; he even felt irritated by the sound which had broken in upon the strange confusion of time in which he found himself. And he felt it was impossible to go into the cottage and interrupt his wife, though he knew she would be glad he had returned to her. But he could not go in. He had the most certain foreknowledge that if he did go in now he would quarrel violently with her. He would invent some excuse to anger him. For he was at war with himself; an intense battle was taking place inside him, and if he met her now he would only drag her into the conflict.

Crossing the field very quickly, his hand shading his eyes against the brilliant light, a burning impatient feeling sending him on, as though he were in pursuit of some enemy, he returned to the village and sat in the bar of the Trevelyan Arms, talking in an absent way to friends there, knowing his wife would be wondering where he was, reluctant to return home till something had been answered.

And now one question clarified itself from the muddle of his thoughts: what had he seen on the occasion of his first walk across the field, ten years ago? A child's face painted on glass? (But *had* there been? Wasn't he confusing the scenes?) A white kitten and a basket with green twine? (Again, was this *certain*?) A woman with golden hair writing by a wood fire? (Yes – surely he had seen her?) A man standing with a saw in his hand, watching the woman through the window – a man intensely happy and proud and full of peace in his soul whose vitality leapt towards the vitality in the woman and the children, born and unborn, as the wild flames of the first autumn fire leapt into the soot-encrusted chimney of the old cottage?

Oh – but had he seen that – *had* he?

Suddenly, from his seat in the now crowded bar, he rose to his feet. The words 'Tyme Tryeth Troth' stared him in the face. 'The illusion we have made of time,' he muttered, 'mocks at and challenges the truth of eternal instant which is at the very heart of all of us.' And then again he thought: a troth is plighted, two hands clasp in the eternal truth; this is not just something that once happened. Like the hands plighted upon the cross of man's intolerable misery, this happened, was happening now. And the false fruit that man had eaten in the garden – was this the fruit of the great illusion? That self-wounding half-knowledge of existence and essence which had crucified man to the unfolding of seasons and the toll of the bell of midnight?

A strange desperate feeling seized him. He wished his lover

were here now. For it was dark, it would take him half an hour
to walk home, and in that time the urgency of what he wanted
to say to her would be lost. Yet to hurry away from here when
he had found no solution to his problem seemed impossible.
Already he hesitated. Somebody was offering him a drink. He
smiled, accepted it, began to chat. And then the question that
he had asked once before came from him.

'You know where we live, up to Kitto's field – Lupin Cottage – tell me, do you remember who was living up there ten
years ago, this time of year?'

The answer was unequivocal. 'Why, old Miss Trewhella.
She had that place for years before you took it over a month or
so back.'

'You're dead sure about that? There was never a young married couple living there, with a baby?'

'No. The old woman lived there nigh on twenty years.'

And now he was hurrying back, bursting with the excitement of new knowledge, desperately anxious to impart his
news to his wife and convey its full meaning to her.

Its full meaning? In the lane, looking up to the moon where
clouds soared in massive sinister shapes, he felt baffled and
cheated. What was the meaning? He would never properly
know. Never now be able to swear that on that first walk across
the field he had indeed seen that family who was himself, his
wife and his son. And all that would now happen – he would
find his wife tired and irritable, angry with him for being out
so long, the food she had cooked spoilt, her spirit wounded by
his thoughtlessness (as she would naturally interpret it). It was
something he knew he would not be able to defeat unless she
herself came out with willing arms to meet him.

The lane was full of ghosts; the damp earth pressed into the
air the mists of the sorrows and joys of many men and women;
the sycamore leaves drifted willingly from their naked stems to
join the trampled leaves of older years, and a straight pillar of
thin smoke rose from the cottage chimney. Against the back
wall which faced the lane the little ash tree stretched its long
branches.

A window above the stairs showed a small light through a thin curtain. Who was in this house? His love, or emptiness? He felt that he did not know, that he might open the gate upon nothing more than memory. There was the long trunk of the apple tree waiting to be sawn. But it might remain there many years, the cottage empty and falling to decay, and nobody would touch that piece of wood. Was he approaching a place where he had once lived with his wife and child? Had all this beauty gone, and was he left alone to remember it?

But there, in the long bright rays of the moon, leaning against the stone lintel of the door, was the woman who loved him.

He did not like to go near her: he could not say anything. And she smiled and stretched out her hands.

'What a lovely night!' she said.

'Yes. You look so beautiful standing there. This evening I saw you writing at the table. And I couldn't come in.'

'Couldn't you, love? Why?'

She smiled, and he came nearer to her, unwilling to touch her, to break the austere beauty of this moment. He almost prayed that she would not move for a long time, not ask him any questions. So he replied, in an indifferent tone, 'Oh, I don't know; just a mood.' And he stood very near her, still not touching her, and thinking again, 'A day will come when this cottage will be empty and the weeds will grow up in the path.'

Then her arms were round him, her head lay on his shoulder and she was stroking his hair. There was nothing, he suddenly realized, to tell her. For she was a person who had reached a strange unconscious union with the mystery of time, and his own doubts would only infect her with bewilderment.

No – there was nothing to say. It was only necessary to remember that his happiness, even though it might be assaulted by the weight of past and future sadness, stood eternally graven upon the tablets of time. In their quiet room where the fire still burnt and the candles were alight he ate the food she brought him and listened to her as she talked of the day's events. They were both very happy. And presently, as they lay in their bed, he took her right hand in his and clasped it, and fell, with her, into sleep. While they slept the west wind rose and the small rain scudded to the window-panes. Autumn was blown away and winter came and in their sleep many seasons passed and came again. The day came when they had to leave this cottage, and that day too passed, becoming one amongst their many shared memories.

Once, in another autumn, this man walked alone across that wide field to a cottage that he knew was empty. And climbing in through one of the windows he stood in the pitch darkness of the large bedroom where ivy trailed down through holes in the roof. He was neither sad nor happy; yet contented; and he knew that he had entered the cottage for the last time.

When his son was a young man his father told him much about their earlier days and quoted the words of the Trevelyan motto. 'There's a very great deal of wisdom in those three words,' he said, 'and I'd like you to remember them.'

The son did not forget them – for who could? And one day with a girl he loved, he found himself in that part of the West country where he had lived for a short while as a child. They walked across a cornfield on a September evening when the sun went slow and red and large down the sky; and climbing a wall lost in brambles and thorns they looked at the crumbling ruins of the cottage. Masses of yellow lupins had spread over the ground.

'This is the place,' said the boy. 'And this is my first memory – do you want me to tell you? It's not really interesting.'

The girl, being in love with him, was interested in everything about him. So he told her.

'I don't really remember the cottage at all. I can't have been more than three and it's all gone from me. But I know we lived here for a time. It was called Lupin Cottage – and there are the lupins – see?'

He stood on the hedge, suddenly growing excited, and taking her hand helped her down to the other side. 'There's something I'm trying to remember,' he said. 'But from here – no, I can't.' He paused and battered his fist impatiently against his forehead. 'We must go inside,' he told her. 'Come on. I shall remember then.'

The padlocked door was choked by a mass of willow herb and nettles. But the glass in the windows was broken and it was easy enough to climb in. Smashing a way through the nettles, he encouraged her to one of the windows. She was not happy about it.

'It doesn't look safe. Need we go in?'

'Yes, we must. Come on.'

Now he was through the window and leaning over to help her inside.

'I don't want to come,' she cried. 'It's horrible in there — dark and smelly and full of spiders.'

'Please — please come. I'm here, aren't I? You can't come to any harm. It's important to us. You must come.'

Suddenly she realized that if she wanted to retain his love for her she would have to follow him wherever he went. Shivering and trembling with fear, she climbed over the sill and joined him inside.

They went upstairs, all the time the boy filled with an excitement she could not properly understand. Then they went into a room where some of the boards were rotted away and the sky showed through the fallen roof. Taking her hand, he led her carefully to the window-seat where great chunks of plaster and slates and laths of worm-dried wood had fallen. He looked through the window to the wide field where the sun shimmered in the corn. And then he gave a great sigh and tears were in his eyes as he clutched her hand tighter.

'Yes, this must have been my room,' he said. 'This is the view I've always wanted of that field. The first thing I can remember, seeing that field from here one evening, about this time, when the sun was setting. Something odd happened, which probably hasn't got any significance; but it's very clear in my memory. I must have got out of bed and stood on this window-seat. I had something in my hand and was tapping the window and looking at the field. It seemed immense — like the whole world. I could see my father in the garden, standing down there with a saw in his hand. And I tried to attract his attention, but he wouldn't look up. I called, I think; but he didn't hear me. Then something happened – what was it?'

He rubbed his left fingers across his eyes and with his right hand still held hers. 'Yes, I remember. It was only this. A man suddenly appeared on the top of the hedge. He was a very old man, or so I remember him; with a grey beard. And he looked terribly tired and miserable. But suddenly he looked up to this window and smiled at me. I remember that smile – it was very sweet and trustful; the sort of way a child would smile. But I was very angry. I wanted my father to look up and smile at me and he wouldn't do so. Then the old man turned and jumped back again into the field; and suddenly my father dropped his saw, climbed over the wall, and started to follow the old man right across the field. I watched them both. The old man was hurrying as though he was scared; and my father was chasing him. I believe he was running. You see right across the field – by those fir trees?'

The girl followed his pointing finger.

'Over there, I could hardly see them, the sun was so bright – my father caught the old man by the shoulders and swung him round and stared at him. Then they disappeared together. That's all I can remember. Doesn't it sound silly?'

The girl looked at him. 'No, it doesn't. Nothing that you tell me about yourself seems silly.'

By the window, overlooking the broad field, these two plighted their troth.